◖ Breathless, Sam clung to Ace. She was surrounded by frightened horses.

The mares boiled toward them, eyes wide.

A big honey-colored mare came right at them. Her breath huffed hot and steamy as her head swung right, then left. Her dark eyes looked confused. At the last minute, her knees lifted and Sam knew she was trying to jump the obstacle before her.

The obstacle was Ace. The mare would never clear a horse and rider. Sam imagined those heavy hooves leaping toward her face.

"No!" Sam shouted, but the mare was lifting off the ground.

If only she could fly, Sam thought.

But she couldn't. Instead of clearing Ace, the big mare slammed into him.

In a tangle of hot horseflesh and leather, Sam hit the desert floor. ◗

Phantom Stallion

7

Desert Dancer

TERRI FARLEY

Caroline's please return

AVON BOOKS

An Imprint of HarperCollinsPublishers

Library of Congress Catalog Card Number:
2002094455
ISBN 0-06-053725-6

First Avon edition, 2003

AVON TRADEMARK REG. U.S. PAT. OFF. AND IN OTHER COUNTRIES,
MARCA REGISTRADA, HECHO EN U.S.A.

Visit us on the World Wide Web!
www.harperchildrens.com

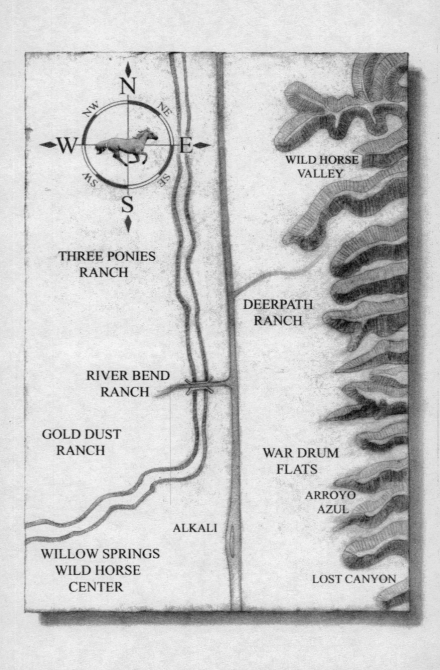

Chapter One

Samantha Forster stood in the shower, listening to the wild neighs and galloping hooves of mustangs. She shook water out of her ears, parted the shower curtains, and stuck her head out.

Her kitten, Cougar, sat on the tile around the bathroom sink, cleaning a paw. His gold eyes met her blue ones.

"Mew?"

Sam knew they were alone in the white two-story house on River Bend Ranch. Gram and Brynna, her soon-to-be stepmother, were in town arranging altar flowers for the wedding and checking the decorations for the reception. Dad and Dallas, River Bend's foreman and Dad's reluctant best man, had driven in to Darton to pick up tuxedos.

Sam kept listening, but when she heard no more whinnies, she relaxed. Her shoulders sagged as she sighed.

"Nothing, Cougar," Sam told the brown kitten. "Only my imagination."

Sam closed the shower curtains and sang. Maybe she could drown her silly thoughts with music.

"Dashing through the snow, in a one-horse open sleigh . . ."

No snow was predicted, but it was Christmas Eve and the carol suited her excited mood.

Six hours from now, bells would ring from the steeple of the white Methodist church in Darton. As maid of honor, she'd move down the aisle toward her smiling father. She'd wear a pine-green gown and carry a bouquet of roses. Minutes later, Brynna Olson, director of the Willow Springs Wild Horse Center, would be married to Wyatt Forster, cattle rancher. Sam would have a stepmother and, strange as she would have thought it just last summer, she liked the idea just fine.

"O'er the fields we go," Sam kept singing. She loved the way her voice echoed in the shower, but it was time to get out. It was after ten A.M. Jake would be here to pick her up at two and there was lots to do before then.

Still, if she hurried, she'd have time to investigate. She had definitely heard something, and since it was December, it shouldn't be wild horses. The mustangs should be tucked away in the Phantom's secret valley. A quick ride would put her mind at rest.

Sam cranked the water off. She'd promised to do

a few last-minute chores before leaving the house. She squeezed the water from her auburn hair, then pushed open the shower curtains, still singing.

". . . laughing all the way—ha ha ha!"

Cougar didn't like that last part. He jumped for the towel rack, clung to a blue terry cloth towel, and swayed there. Looking over his shoulder, he watched Sam for further signs of insanity.

When her dripping hand reached in his direction, he fell skittering to the floor. Sam opened the bathroom door so he could escape.

There it was again. Through the opening, she heard a confusion of high-pitched neighs that didn't belong anywhere near River Bend.

Dressed in a towel, Sam sprinted to her bedroom window and let her eyes search the terrain below.

To her right lay the ten-acre pasture filled with five saddle horses and two mustangs-in-training for the Horse and Rider Protection program. Though their ears pricked forward, listening as if they'd heard the neighs, too, the River Bend horses weren't eager to look into the disturbance. They clustered together, tails to the cold morning wind.

Around the house, the ranch yard was a pale sandy apron. Except for their Border collie, Blaze, sniffing around for breakfast, the yard was empty. She looked toward the bridge over the La Charla River. From there, the road led to Darton if you turned right, to Jake's Three Ponies Ranch if you turned left. There wasn't a car or truck in sight.

Far out over the range, nothing moved except a single crow, flapping across the blue-gray sky.

No matter which direction she stared, nothing looked out of place.

Sam knew what any outsider would say. Seven horses grazed in the big pasture. Two more were stabled in barn stalls. If she heard neighs, they had to come from these horses. But she knew that wasn't so . . .

Sam recognized the voice of each horse on River Bend Ranch. She wasn't hearing Ace's high, soaring call, coaxing her to go for a ride, or Strawberry's cranky snorting. The sounds resembled Dark Sunshine's longing whinnies toward the Calico Mountains, but the buckskin mare couldn't make all the overlapping sounds Sam had heard.

Just because she couldn't see anything out of the ordinary didn't mean everything was fine. Jake had accused her of trying to be a horse psychic. That was ridiculous, but Sam and the magnificent stallion called the Phantom definitely shared a connection.

Since summer, his herd had been in turmoil. First, the Phantom had been accused of stealing domestic mares, and a reward had been posted for his capture. The wild bunch had been pursued by rustlers, then left without a leader when the Phantom had been used as a bucking bronc in a rodeo. Just a few weeks ago, an orphaned cougar had stalked the Phantom's herd, hoping to make a meal of a spring foal.

But the young cougar had been captured and transplanted to another mountain range. What could have the horses stirred up now?

Just feet from Sam's window, a second crow crossed the sky, cawing a warning.

"That's it," Sam muttered. She'd jet through her chores, saddle Ace, check things out, and still be back here in time to meet Jake.

Sam dressed as fast as she could, then set to work. She watered the herbs in Gram's window garden, made up the bed for Aunt Sue, who was coming from San Francisco for the wedding, and cleaned up her breakfast dishes.

She dashed from the house, collected the hens' eggs, and made sure all the stock had been fed and watered. She turned Sweetheart into the new round pen next to the barn, but left Ace in his stall.

"I'll be back for you in a minute, good boy." She kissed his muzzle, then ran to refill Blaze's water dish. The Border collie looked toward the front gate and whined.

Sam listened for the horses. Nothing. Blaze rarely fretted over horses, anyway, unless there was a new animal to inspect. Now, he was probably concerned by all the unusual comings and goings.

"Don't worry, Blaze," she said, as the dog licked her hand. "They'll all be back."

Eventually, she almost added, but Blaze wouldn't understand.

After the wedding, Dad and Brynna were leaving for their honeymoon in San Francisco, where they'd stay in Aunt Sue's apartment. Gram was riding with them to the Reno Airport, then flying out to spend Christmas with a friend in New Mexico. Aunt Sue would drive home with Sam and stay most of winter vacation. But that was too much to explain to a dog.

With her outdoor chores finished, Sam ran to the barn for Ace.

The bay gelding stretched his head over the rails of his corral and greeted her with a low rumbling sound. He tossed his black mane from his eyes, baring the white star on his forehead.

"Hey pretty boy," Sam crooned as she saddled him. "Want to go for a quick ride?" As if he understood, the gelding bobbed his head. Sam smoothed her hand over the freeze brand on his neck. Ace was her friend, but he was also a mustang. If she had trouble finding the wild horses, he'd do it for her.

Sam ground-tied Ace just outside the front door, retrieved the basket of eggs she'd left on the porch, and ran inside.

"Eggs in the refrigerator," she muttered to herself. What would Aunt Sue think if there were no eggs for Christmas breakfast?

Fidgeting, Sam found a pencil and made herself reread the list posted on the refrigerator door. She crossed off everything except for the reminder to return a phone call from their neighbor Linc Slocum.

Call Linc about Home on the Range, Gram had written. After that, she'd drawn three question marks.

Sam shook her head.

"No way," she muttered.

Linc Slocum could wait by the phone until next Christmas. Twice, he'd conspired to capture the Phantom. Sam was polite to him in public, but if Home on the Range was another of Linc's business schemes, she wanted no part of it.

She tried not to say "no" to people she loved, but she could stand firm against her enemies.

Time to go. Sam started to grab her old brown Stetson from the peg by the door. She touched her damp hair and decided against it. This was one day she'd go without her hat. Brynna was a horsewoman herself, and pretty good-natured, but she probably wouldn't understand if her maid of honor showed up with hat hair.

It only took Sam half an hour to find two mares from the Phantom's herd. Ace's body vibrated with a low nicker as he caught their scent.

Sam drew rein, making Ace stay back as she searched the brush for wild horses. A flash of red caught her eye, but it wasn't the tiger dun mare who always led the Phantom's band. As her eyes separated the mustangs from the terrain, she recognized two blood bays who always ran and grazed together.

The pair glanced up. Their eyes rolled, showing

white around the dark irises. They were only jumpy, not panicked. Because Sam approached without shouting or swinging a rope, the mustangs bumped shoulders and dismissed her as a threat. Then they went back to lipping the sparse winter grass.

This didn't make sense. There had to be better forage elsewhere. And where was the rest of the band? Wild horses depended on their herd for safety.

"What are you guys doing out here alone?" Sam asked.

Although they'd accepted her before, Sam's voice spooked the mares. Hooves crunched on rocky soil as they broke into a trot, glancing back at her. One mare started toward the highway, head high, mane blowing. Then she changed her mind and both bolted toward War Drum Flats.

Ace gathered himself to gallop, but Sam kept him at a lope. Given a little space, the mares might line out toward the rest of the herd.

They did. The Phantom's mares were scattered all over War Drum Flats. Usually, they stuck together, in case danger made a quick escape necessary.

About a dozen mustangs moved aimlessly along the edge of the small lake on War Drum Flats. She'd bet this was the bunch she'd heard neighing. They were uncharacteristically noisy for a wild band, nickering and snorting as they jostled each other.

What's going on? Sam wondered.

Mustangs were usually silent. Flicked ears might

signal interest in an unfamiliar animal or tell a herd-mate to look at something interesting. Tossed heads could mean irritation or a change in direction. The most violent battle between stallions could be triggered by a hoof pawing the dust. So why were these wild horses so vocal?

Sam glanced up the hill, squinting toward the stair-step mesas. The Phantom was up there somewhere, watching from his lookout.

Even without him, Sam knew his herd. Besides the two blood bay mares, she recognized buckskin, sorrel, and honey chestnut mares. That old bay was one she'd noticed before, too, but where was the lead mare?

As her eyes searched for the red dun with slanting stripes on her forelegs, Sam noticed most of the mustangs were wet and muddy. A gang of five young horses, leggy and full of themselves, splashed knee-deep in the lake, ignoring the calls of their nervous mothers.

A bay colt with a patch of white over one eye seemed to be the ringleader.

"He looks like a little pirate, doesn't he, Ace?" Sam asked the gelding.

Ace only stamped as the colt swooped after the other youngsters, churning the lake white.

Sam shaded her eyes against the winter sun and watched. They were having fun, but the frolicking colts and fillies were spring foals, the most vulnerable members of the herd. Sam understood their mothers' worry.

There were no biting insects this time of year, so the horses couldn't be rolling in mud to protect themselves from bites. And the lake was as full as it ever got, so the mares and foals wouldn't have to wade out to drink. Why would the lead mare let them walk into the lake, where they were slowed by the mud and exposed to predators?

Shaggy with winter hair, the horses looked almost prehistoric. Beneath their wet coats, Sam could see their ribs. When Jake picked her up, she'd have to ask if that was normal for this time of year.

Jake. How long did she have before he showed up at River Bend? Sam glanced at her wrist. In her hurry to get dressed, she'd forgotten to strap on her watch, but she should have plenty of time.

Sam focused on each horse individually. At a rough count, there must be at least thirty animals, but the red dun had always been easy to spot. Although she was small and delicate, gliding over the desert like a doe, she had attitude.

The dun was always alert, always in the lead. Sam remembered how she'd backed down the hammerhead stallion who'd tried to steal the Phantom's mares. When the Phantom had been captured and his son Moon had appointed himself leader of the band, the red dun had kept her distance. Sam always had the feeling the dun allowed the young black stallion to practice being boss, though she was really in charge.

There was a squeal from the lake as the colt with the white eye patch bit one of his playmates. Sam looked the bunch over again. They were all babies. No more than six months old.

She was sure she'd spotted every single horse except the Phantom and his lead mare.

"Where are they, Ace?" Sam leaned low, pressing her cheek against her gelding's warm neck. If someone wanted to put the herd in even more turmoil, getting rid of the top-ranking horses would do it.

All at once, she felt Ace tighten. He flung his head high and his nostrils quivered in a silent greeting. The Phantom was coming down from the mountain.

Moving with such grace that he seemed to float, the stallion left the ridge, following the switchback trails that crisscrossed the mountainside.

The red dun mare might be missing, but the herd could depend on their leader.

Sam sighed. Everything would be okay. It was time to get back to River Bend, so that she wouldn't have to hear Jake's nagging.

When the mares noticed the stallion, they surged toward him. Just as they did, a motorcycle passed on the highway and the herd panicked.

A dozen frantic neighs rose and the young horses in the lake responded by splashing toward shore.

"Oh no." Sam sucked in a breath. Caught

between the mares and their young, she wasn't sure what to do. "Okay, Ace, it's up to you."

Sam loosened her reins. Ace didn't want to be caught between the two bunches of horses any more than she did. He sprinted along the lakeshore, running for home.

She glanced over her shoulder. The mares were racing after their colts, not about to let their babies get away. Most of the young horses ran ahead of Ace, tails streaming. A few ran beside him, matching his strides, mindless of their mothers' pursuit.

Breathless, Sam clung to Ace. She was surrounded by frightened horses. Her face was lashed by Ace's flying mane. She felt his strong, short legs thrust forward and pull back. Forward, back. Two colts swerved around a boulder, collided with Ace's shoulder, and kept galloping. They didn't know how to escape what had scared them. In fact, Sam knew they'd already forgotten the sound. The young horses were simply running scared.

For one nightmare instant, Sam thought of her accident from years ago. She could fall again. First she'd lose her grip on the reins. Next, she'd bounce free of the saddle. Then, she'd be tumbling in slow motion, hit the ground, and lose consciousness. But this time she wouldn't be struck by one hoof from one horse.

It had happened before. It could happen again.

Ace's choppy gait told Sam the gelding felt her

fear. She needed to knock that off. The little gelding was doing his best for her. She had to return his effort.

Sam firmed her legs against Ace. She kept her hands quiet on the reins and settled her boots deeper into her stirrups. She would not fall. Ace had to know she was in control. Everything would be all right. She could keep her seat if she wasn't scared.

Ace settled into a steady run, letting all the wild-eyed colts but one stampede past.

Sam looked down on the soft bay coat alongside Ace. The patch-eyed colt didn't look like a little pirate now. He looked scared and weary.

Above the pounding hooves, Sam heard a mare call out. Then another. The mothers must have said something calming, because the young horses slowed.

All except for the little bay. He rammed into those ahead of him and stumbled.

Ace swerved left, trying not to step on the youngster. His turn brought him face-to-face with a second group of horses.

The mares boiled toward them, eyes wide.

A big honey-colored mare came right at them. Her breath huffed hot and steamy as her head swung right, then left. Her dark eyes looked confused. At the last minute, her knees lifted and Sam knew she was trying to jump the obstacle before her.

The obstacle was Ace. The mare would never clear a horse and rider. Sam imagined those heavy hooves leaping toward her face.

"No!" Sam shouted, but the mare was lifting off the ground.

If only she could fly, Sam thought.

But she couldn't. Instead of clearing Ace, the big mare slammed into him.

In a tangle of hot horseflesh and leather, Sam hit the desert floor.

Chapter Two

$\mathcal{A}$ce fell to his knees. Sam pitched forward, then sideways, but stayed astride. She kicked free of her right stirrup. She'd seen Jake's ruined leg after a horse pinned it to the ground. She feared shattered bones more than stampeding horses.

Ace was falling. She had to get off. Maybe he could scramble up, without her flailing weight. He tried to and for an instant she clung to the saddle horn, hopping alongside her horse.

Sam's boots scuffled on the ground, trying to keep up. She made her fingers release their grip on the saddle horn. At last she stood flat-footed, but her knees were trembling as a paint mare struck her left shoulder, spinning her around.

The Phantom trumpeted a command. Sam couldn't tell where the sound came from, but it rang loud and demanding. A blue-gray horse sideswiped her with such impact, Sam fell on the seat of her jeans.

Her teeth clacked together. Her kneecaps locked and Sam sat facing the herd. They parted around her, thundering hooves shaking her insides.

She pulled her heels back toward her. Why couldn't she stand? She was too shaken to do anything but stare at the marks her bootheels had gouged in the dirt. Finally, she curled into a crouch with her arms crossed over her head.

In the seconds since she'd left the saddle, Ace had lurched to his feet and was swept on by the irresistible tide of horses. He called once, but then he was gone and she knew she had to do the same thing. Stand.

Get up! Her mind screamed, but she couldn't leave her crouch.

Get up! She squinted against bright splashes of light interrupted by running horses.

If she stayed down, the horses would try to jump her.

Get up or get your brains kicked out. That thought got her up. The herd split, going around her like a river passes boulders in its path.

Sam still stood when the last horse galloped past. She staggered a step into the quiet they'd left behind. But where was she going? She felt hot and dizzy, and there was no reason she couldn't, just for a minute, lie down.

She did. Her cheek rested right there on cold dirt cut by many hooves. Her chest heaved and her eyes closed. She couldn't hear her own breathing because the thunder of hooves had left her ears ringing.

She wasn't hurt. She wasn't in shock, just—Sam admitted to herself—really scared. She'd been so certain a hoof would strike her head again. So positive she'd wake up in a white hospital bed, just like before.

She felt weak. *I want my Dad*, she thought. *I want Jake or Gram or somebody to be with me.*

Suddenly, shade fell over her, blocking the watery winter sunlight.

Right next to her head, beneath a coating of dust, stood hooves that shone like pewter. Above the hooves, she saw trim fetlocks.

Sam blinked, opening her eyes wider. Pale equine legs, grayed with dirt, were planted four-square around her. Sam sighed, closing her eyes to enjoy her dream.

"Zanzibar," she whispered, calling him by the secret name known only to the two of them.

The stallion answered with a low nicker. He was solid, dependable, and no dream at all. He meant to protect her, but he was a wild horse. There was no telling what he'd do if a sudden sound startled him or a rival stallion appeared on the horizon.

"Hey, boy," Sam said. She trembled and the stallion was steady, but this was not a safe position and she knew it. "I'd be an idiot to try to make you move, wouldn't I, good horse? When you're good and ready, you'll walk away."

And then, he did. The stallion moved off, before

turning and lowering his head.

"You really look like a wild horse today, fella."

The stallion's silver coat showed smears of dirt and patches where sweat had dried and left his hair stiff. Ropey white mane clumped on his neck and his brown eyes glowed with intelligence. Concern showed as clearly in his eyes as if he'd been a human.

His muzzle came toward Sam and he whuffled his lips over her hair.

"I'm fine," she told him. "I bet you're having a hard time keeping everyone together without your lead mare. Is that why you look so scruffy?"

Even with no one else to hear, Sam felt guilty saying that to such a kingly animal. But he looked weary. It was a lead mare's job to find water and good graze and maintain discipline. The red dun would have kept the herd in the secret wild horse valley.

Every minute Zanzibar watched over her, he'd have farther to run to catch up with the herd. And they'd been running toward the highway.

As Sam sat up, the stallion backed out of reach, swinging his head to the side to keep an eye on her.

"You like me fine, but I'm still a human. Is that it?" Sam crooned to the mustang.

His head jerked upward, scattering his thick forelock away from his eyes.

Sam touched the scratchy horsehair bracelet around her wrist and saw his eyes follow her movement. She sighed.

"You'd better go after your herd." Sam moved to get up.

He trotted a few steps in the direction the horses had fled, then bolted after them.

Sam felt achy all over. Just a few weeks ago, a cougar's pounce had knocked her off Strawberry. She still had a few bruises.

She wasn't that bad a rider. She'd been raised on a ranch. She'd ridden since she was two years old. Since the accident, though, she'd fallen a lot.

On the day of the accident, the Phantom had been a two-year-old she called Blackie. He'd just been learning the feel of a saddle and rider, when he'd become trapped while passing through a gate. She'd been on his back. Blackie's bucking had thrown her to the ground. In his hurry to escape, he'd accidentally kicked her head and she'd been in a coma for days.

Sam tried to count the times she'd fallen since then, but she felt sick to her stomach. She'd been back on the ranch for seven months. She should be an expert rider, but she was barely competent.

Enough.

All at once, Sam realized she was out of time. She couldn't be standing out in the middle of the desert, moping over her clumsy riding ability when her clean hair was dirty again and the wedding march would be booming from the church pipe organ soon.

Of course she didn't know how soon, because

she'd left her watch at home. Worse than all that, Jake would be pulling his father's truck into the ranch yard to pick her up any minute now.

Jake Ely had been her friend since childhood, but he was three years older and considered himself her big brother. Ever since she'd fallen from the Phantom, Jake had thought she needed protection. If she told him the truth about her dirty hair and clothes, he'd turn into a human guard dog. Again.

Of course, that assumed she'd get home in time to meet him before the wedding. She'd better do something to make that possible.

Sam started jogging. She winced at the pain in her poor abused body. She wished she was wearing sneakers instead of these heavy leather boots. But she kept going.

Sam had run about a mile when she made out a solitary horse searching for grass near the highway.

Sam ran faster. *Please let it be Ace.*

"Ace?" she called.

The horse's head came up. He watched her approach, moving so that she could see a saddle on his back.

It had to be Ace, but why wasn't he coming to her? Dad always said Ace acted like a pet. She *was* out of breath. Maybe he hadn't recognized her voice.

"Ace!" Sam shouted.

She was close enough now to see the white star on his forehead and the light hair from the freeze brand on his neck. Of course it was Ace! If they hurried, she might be home in time to meet Jake. Sam really hoped so. Jake got crazy when things didn't go the way he'd planned.

"Come here, boy," she called to the gelding.

Ace just stared at her, swishing his tail and chewing like a cow.

"Ace!" Sam stormed toward her horse. "How can you eat lunch at a time like this?"

Reins trailing, Ace trotted away. His eyes rolled white as if she were a monster.

"Oh, no you don't!" Sam shouted. As she sprinted after him, the gelding broke into a lope. "Ace, no!"

She'd never catch up with him now. Why had she let him see her irritation?

Ace hadn't pulled a trick like this since June. On her first cattle drive he'd tried every stunt he knew to make her look like a dude.

"Why now?" she called after him. "Why did you have to pick my father's wedding day to act like you've been eating loco weed?"

Maybe Ace took pity on her. Maybe the mention of eating reminded him she was the keeper of his oats. Whatever it was, something clicked in his equine brain. Ace did a U-turn and trotted back to nuzzle her hands as if he'd missed her more than he could express.

"You can apologize later," Sam said as the horse blinked his innocent brown eyes. "Right now, I want you to act like Pegasus and fly to River Bend before Jake gets there."

They almost made it.

From across the range, Sam spotted a truck the color of old blue jeans, crossing the bridge into the ranch yard. At the same time, Ace made a grunting sound as if she'd run him too hard.

Sam sucked in a breath. She knew Ace was fine. She'd bet he was just having a stubborn day, but she refused to take a chance. Jake would already be mad, she thought, snugging her reins. She spared her horse and hoped Jake was so dressed up for his role as usher, he wouldn't do anything stupid.

As soon as they trotted into the ranch yard, Jake burst out of the truck and swooped down on her like a vengeful hawk. He wore a pressed blue shirt that actually buttoned down the front and pants that weren't jeans. His black hair was slick and neat.

She barely had time to notice how nice he looked. When he reached her, she'd just dismounted. He crowded her, standing about a foot away. His hands were clenched in fists and they moved in short jerks at his sides, as if he was trying to keep from strangling her.

"This is the last time, Samantha!" he roared, then jerked his head toward the truck.

Okay, if Jake wanted to yell, she could match him.

"The last time that what?" Sam shouted back.

Ace sidled away, eyes rolling all over again, as if he'd known she'd turn into a beast, some time.

The best defense was a good offense, Sam thought. She had no time to explain it to Ace, but she knew Jake had no respect for people who just rolled over and played dead when they were challenged. Her number-one rule in dealing with Jake was to stand firm, even if she was wrong.

Jake's glare turned into something dangerous. Sam swallowed hard and wondered if today might be an exception to her rule.

Just how late am I? Sam wondered.

Jake drew a deep breath, shouldered past her, and began stripping the tack from Ace.

"Get in the truck," he ordered, without turning around.

"I'm just going to run inside and take a quick shower," Sam began. "I have to wash my hair."

"No," Jake said. He slung Ace's saddle over a fence rail. "I'm not letting you out of my sight."

Because she'd heard him make that sort of silly vow a dozen times before, Sam relaxed a little.

Jake was nervous about the wedding, not mad at her. Although today might not be a good day to stand toe-to-toe arguing, she could still get what she wanted. She made her voice quiet and reasonable.

"My hair is dirty," Sam explained. "I can't get in the truck until I've taken a shower. I'm sure you understand."

"There's no time," he said. He removed Ace's bridle and pumped some fresh water into the trough so the horse could drink.

"Of course there's time," Sam told him, calmly. "While you put Ace up I can run upstairs, wash my hair, and be ready to go in ten minutes."

"Ace can put himself up." Jake slapped the bay's rump and he trotted toward the barn. "And your hair's fine."

Jake walked toward the truck as if he expected her to march along behind him. Even then, Sam tried to sound tranquil.

"Now, Jake . . ."

He wheeled around, pointing his index finger her way.

"I don't know what you think you're doing, Samantha, but you can stop talking to me that way. I'm not a bull pawing the ground, about to charge."

"Coulda fooled me," Sam muttered.

Jake closed his eyes for a minute. When he opened them, he didn't look any more peaceful, but he spoke slowly and clearly. "You need to get in the truck and let me drive to the church. Now."

Sam sighed. He was the one wasting time. "Jake, have you looked at my hair?"

"If I hear one more word about your hair . . ." Jake began, but he didn't finish the threat. Instead, he began lecturing her. "They arranged it so you didn't have to remember anything. Your dress, shoes, all your makeup and fancy gear are at the church. That's what Brynna told me. Your Aunt Sue's even bringing a beautician or something, isn't that what you said?"

Sam nodded.

"All you had to do was show up. And I was going to help you with that. You coulda just sat on the porch until I got here, but you couldn't even manage that."

"Why are you so mad?" Sam asked. She grabbed Jake's wrist and turned it so she could see his watch. "We've got time. I'm only ten minutes late."

Sam could hear the amazement in her own voice. Maybe that was what pushed Jake over the edge.

"Why am I so mad? Let's see. Could it be 'cause you're making both of us seem like careless kids?" Jake squared his shoulders and drew up to his full height. "I'm sixteen. I drive. I earn money for training horses. I don't need you making me look bad . . . and speaking of looking bad," Jake said, really focusing on her for the first time. "What happened to you?"

Sam wanted to scream. She'd been telling him she had to shower, hadn't she? Now he wanted the whole story, but she was pretty sure he wouldn't like it.

"I was riding along, minding my own business," she began.

"You can tell me while we drive," he said, and pointed at the truck.

She was not about to be ordered around like a puppy.

"I'm not getting in that truck 'til my hair is clean." Sam planted her feet. She was trying to stare him down when she realized he was carefully rolling up his sleeves.

"Bend over," he said.

"What?"

Jake didn't push very hard, but because she was surprised, Sam found herself on her knees beside the horse trough as Jake pumped water over her head.

She came up sputtering and furious. She heard her own yowl, which sounded like a wet cat, but she didn't care. Jake Ely was going to pay for this.

"Now your hair's clean. Let's go."

Teeth chattering, Sam did as she was told. Arms crossed and eyes narrowed, she vibrated with anger. She was a really nice person. She never hurt anyone and she rarely planned revenge, but she was about to make an exception for Jake Ely.

Chapter Three

Sam burst into the dressing room off the church sanctuary. This was where she was supposed to meet Gram and Brynna, but the room looked empty.

It wasn't. Dressed in yards of white lace, Brynna stood alone, facing a mirror. She looked like a fairy-tale princess, but she also looked very lonely.

As Brynna turned, Sam began babbling excuses.

"I'm so sorry I'm late. And that I look like a drowned rat." Sam touched her hair, but Brynna's relieved expression told her not to jump into a long explanation blaming Jake. "I didn't mean to make you worry."

Smiling, Brynna rustled toward Sam.

"This is how it's going to be, isn't it?" Brynna asked. She plucked a tissue from a box and gently wiped Sam's cheek.

Sam wasn't sure what Brynna meant, but the remark made her feel like a child. It didn't help that her face was dirty because she'd actually settled down for a nap on the desert floor. Wow. She should have been worrying about her head, not her hair.

"It's a long story," Sam admitted.

"I just bet," Brynna said. Her smile was lopsided as her fingertips skimmed over Sam's hair.

The gesture reminded Sam of the way hens scratched at something they weren't sure they should eat.

"I know." Sam moaned, but Brynna didn't look disheartened.

"Don't worry. Even though it's too late for a manicure," Brynna said, holding up her own silvery white nails, "the girl your Aunt Sue found to help us out can work miracles with hair."

Brynna twirled so Sam could see that her businesslike French braid had been replaced with a cascade of curls, dotted with white velvet flowers.

"It's so pretty," Sam said, but Brynna was opening the dressing room door and peeking out. She motioned, trying to get someone's attention. When that didn't work, Brynna put two fingers to her lips and gave an ear-splitting cowgirl whistle.

Sam couldn't help laughing. So much for the fairy-tale bride. Brynna swirled around with a sheepish grin. "Well, everyone was busy, and I had to get Callie's attention."

"Callie?"

"The hair girl your Aunt Sue hired," Brynna explained. "You must not have passed her as you came in, because you'd have noticed her. She has a pierced nose and her hair's a shade of yellow that doesn't occur naturally in human beings."

Now Brynna really didn't sound like a princess. She sounded like the biologist she was.

"Where is Aunt Sue?" Sam asked. Though she'd lived for two whole years with Aunt Sue while recovering from her riding accident, they'd only talked on the phone since Sam had moved back to Nevada seven months ago.

Aunt Sue was a teacher, and now that it was school vacation for both of them, she would stay with Sam while Dad and Brynna honeymooned.

"Sue is helping your gram with the buffet," Brynna said.

Sam thought Brynna looked a little skeptical, as if she were about to say something else.

Aunt Sue was short in height, but never short of opinions, and she did have a way of taking over.

But Brynna only shook her head and smiled. "It's really nice of her to let us use her apartment while she visits with you."

Sam knew Aunt Sue's arrival was more than a visit, but she bit her tongue to keep from asking Brynna why Dad wouldn't leave her alone. Even though she was thirteen years old, he couldn't get over the idea she needed a baby-sitter.

The sudden chords of the pipe organ surged through the room.

"That's our cue," Brynna said, drawing a deep

breath. "We've got half an hour before the ceremony. Plenty of time," she said as she helped Sam into a special slip with a flounced petticoat. "Now, tell me what happened to make you late? I know it had to do with horses. Did you take another fall?"

Another fall. Even Brynna had noticed. Sam felt a hot blush cover her face. For a minute, she wanted to confide in Brynna. But this was Brynna's wedding day. It would be selfish to wonder aloud why she'd regressed into a lousy, fearful rider.

Besides, she needed Brynna's help with the mustangs.

"More like an emergency dismount," Sam admitted, feeling better when Brynna laughed.

"You're okay, right?" Brynna's glance gave Sam a quick once-over.

"I'm fine, but I'm worried. They stampeded, just because a noise startled them. The Phantom's lead mare is missing and the herd is all confused."

"Missing?" Brynna shook her head with a little grimace. "Remind me what the mare looks like."

"A red dun with tiger stripes on her front legs and—"

"Right." Brynna nodded, and though she appeared to be watching Sam put on light makeup, Brynna's eyes looked far away. "She's the one that was scolding Moon when we saw the herd up in Lost Canyon. She didn't look old or unhealthy," Brynna mused.

Sam's spirits fell. She'd hoped Brynna would have a logical explanation for the dun's absence. "Could the wranglers have brought her in?"

"I doubt it," Brynna said. "We did so many gathers in the late summer and early fall, because of the drought, we haven't needed to do more."

That left injury or death as reasons for the mare's disappearance. Sam's chest felt heavy.

"When was the last time you saw her?" Brynna asked. "There's a slight chance she left the herd to foal, then got left behind. But that's so unlikely, Sam. I wouldn't want you to count on it."

"I saw her a couple weeks ago. She looked slim and fast," Sam said. "She couldn't have been carrying a foal."

"Listen, I've been busy getting my Willow Springs work done, so Wyatt and I could get away," Brynna sounded suddenly more upbeat. "If an injured or feral horse was brought in, I might not know about it. After the ceremony, I'll put in a call to my substitute—" Brynna broke off with a wry smile. "You know who he is, don't you?"

"Oh, my gosh." Sam groaned. "Tell me it's not Norman White."

"I could, but I'd be lying. *Mr.* White is covering for me this week."

Sam ignored Brynna's gentle reprimand because, really, he didn't deserve her respect. Once before Norman White had filled in for Brynna. The bossy bureaucrat had tried to "tie up loose ends" by putting down mustangs he classified as "unadoptable."

Luckily, Mrs. Allen, their neighbor, had taken the horses in and started the Blind Faith Mustang Sanctuary.

Sam didn't look forward to meeting up with Norman White again, but she'd do anything for the Phantom and his herd.

"Anyway," Brynna went on. "Since you're acquainted with Mr. White, I'll notify him that you're looking for the mare. Tomorrow's Christmas, so you can't go then, but maybe Jake can drive you up the day after."

"I don't think so," Sam said. By the time she settled her grudge against Jake, the only place he'd want to drive her would be to the sheriff's office.

"Your Aunt Sue, then," Brynna said as a knock sounded on the dressing room door. "Come in."

The girl who sauntered in had gray eyes behind wire-framed granny glasses. Her hair curved in a chrome-yellow page boy. Sam's mind churned, trying to decide why she looked familiar.

"Mmmm, it smells heavenly in here. The flowers must've arrived, " the girl said.

Above a long, gauzy skirt she wore a black tee-shirt featuring a heart drawn to look like hot-pink barbed wire. Sam guessed that was in tribute to the wedding.

"They have," Brynna said, pointing to bouquets

of tiny white roses and fresh pine. "Callie, this is my daughter-to-be, Samantha Forster. Sam, this is Callie—" Brynna paused.

"Thurston," the girl supplied her last name. "I recognize you. We rode the bus together."

"Right," Sam said. How could Callie be both a student and a hairdresser?

"You commune with the white stallion," Callie said.

Commune? Sam loved the Phantom, but *commune* sounded paranormal, as if she could read his mind.

"I wish that were true," Sam said, smiling. "I think about him plenty, but I don't know how often he thinks about me."

It was a lame response, but Callie didn't seem to notice. She walked around Sam, calculating the damage she'd done to her auburn hair.

Wind. Dirt. Horse trough water. Sam figured she'd look better if she wore her Stetson down the aisle, but Callie didn't appear overwhelmed. In fact, she looked like she'd just accepted a dare as she plugged in a curling iron, grabbed a brush, and considered Sam with anticipation.

"It turns out that Callie is going to be one of our adopters," Brynna said as she looked in the mirror to straighten her veil.

"That's great! Congratulations," Sam said, but she'd just gotten a good look at one of Callie's professional tools. Callie held a brush bristling with plastic spikes. She held it in the air, ready to subdue Sam's unruly hair. Maybe she could distract her. "Tell me about your horse."

"I will," Callie promised. "I hope I can connect with her like you do with the Phantom."

"It takes time," Sam began.

"Which we don't have much of, right now," Brynna reminded the girls.

"Right," Callie said, closing in with the brush.

"Oh, yeah. Sorry," Sam added, but over the scream of the hair dryer, no one heard her.

The church glowed with candlelight as Sam moved down the aisle. Her nerves disappeared when she saw Dad. He must have looked handsome. Everyone said so later, but all Sam knew was that his eyes were full of her and he was proud. She wanted to run down the aisle and hug him. Instead, she acted her age, taking one measured step after the other, just as she'd done in rehearsal.

After that, the wedding passed in a blur.

Dallas dropped the gold ring he was passing to Dad. A soloist sang an old Beatles song about loving each other 'til they were sixty-four. Brynna caught her heel in the hem of her wedding dress, tripped, and Dad caught her and kissed her before the minister pronounced them married. As the ceremony ended with a joyous hymn, Dad and Brynna led the way back down the aisle. Sam took Dallas's arm and they followed along.

All the guests in the church pews looked happy, especially Aunt Sue, who wore a red suit and jerked her thumb skyward as she gave Sam a huge smile.

The organist played so loudly, Sam almost didn't hear Dallas say, "That's it, then. Head 'em up and move 'em out."

A Western swing band played in the crowded reception hall. Some guests juggled plates of finger food while others danced, drank sparkling cider, and agreed this was the liveliest Christmas Eve they'd ever seen.

Now Sam was waiting for her best friend, Jen. They'd made a deal to meet at the punch bowl once the reception began.

Jen and her mother were spending most of winter vacation with cousins in Utah and this would be the last chance Sam had to hang around with Jen before she left.

But Aunt Sue found her first.

"Sam, honey, I have missed you so much." Aunt Sue swept her up in a hug scented with perfume and hairspray. "My apartment is just empty without you."

Sam knew she'd have a lipstick kiss on her cheek, but she didn't care. Aunt Sue lit up the room in her bright suit and silver-blond hair. If she looked teary, it was just for a moment, and her smile never wavered.

Sam wondered if that was how Mom would have looked, seeing her daughter in her first formal dress?

"No matter. We have all week together," Aunt Sue said, brushing aside her melancholy. Then she nodded toward the buffet where Gram was urging people to fill their plates. "Grace tells me we'll have the house to ourselves. She's taking a Southwestern cooking class with a friend, right? It's just as well," she said, lowering her voice. "I brought plenty of videos and junk food. I don't think Grace would approve."

Sam laughed. She was just about to praise Aunt Sue's contribution to their vacation fun, when Linc Slocum's voice boomed over the music.

"Didn't take that little lady long to put her lasso on Wyatt," Slocum said. "She's got him trussed up and hog-tied good and proper."

Startled guests stared, then saw who was talking and looked away.

Most neighbors had gotten used to the rich man who'd proven he'd pay lots of money to be accepted as a real Westerner. His strategy hadn't worked, but his movie cowboy clothes and speech were hard to miss.

"My, that gentleman certainly is dressed for the occasion." Aunt Sue was polite, but Sam could hear the laughter bubbling under her words.

From the front, Linc's attire looked almost sedate. He wore a black Western coat and slacks with a white shirt. His diamond-eyed steer's head bolo tie was a little flashy, but not bad for Slocum.

Then he turned around. The back of his jacket squirmed with embroidery. Orange and purple roosters fought in a blizzard of floating feathers and glittering red sequins that looked a lot like blood.

"Please notice he's the only one here wearing . . ." Sam began.

"Duly noted," Aunt Sue said, then peered into the punch bowl. "All but empty," she observed, tsking. "No rest for the wicked. I'd better return to my duties, but find me after all the festivities," she told Sam, "because I'm your ride and you'll have to show me how to drive to *the ranch*." Aunt Sue gave a theatrical shudder.

"Aunt Sue, you'll love River Bend," Sam insisted.

"Samantha, this is one way in which I am quite different from your mother. Louise, bless her silly little heart, believed scorpions, bloodthirsty coyotes, and steely-eyed cowpokes were romantic. She always wanted to live on a ranch. I, on the other hand, find elevators, crowded sidewalks, and cable cars exciting. I always wanted to live in civilization."

"By the end of the week, you won't want to leave," Sam promised.

"We'll see, honey," Aunt Sue kissed Sam's cheek again and disappeared toward the church kitchen.

Sam wished Jen would hurry. Their meeting place was too crowded with Slocums. Because Dad and Brynna were good neighbors, the entire Slocum family had been invited.

While Linc boomed out folksy expressions, Rachel looked bored and Ryan accepted Nevada-style welcomes.

Most members of the ranch families knew Rachel, Linc's beautiful and snobby daughter, but many were taking their first look at her twin from England, and seemed dazzled by how different Ryan Slocum was from his father.

Sam was watching from the corner of her eye, trying not to stare, when Jen appeared beside her.

"Are you checking this out?" Jen nodded toward Ryan and his audience.

Jen looked pretty in a blue velvet jumper over a silky white turtleneck, but the twist of her lips was even more sarcastic than usual.

"They love it when he tilts his head and gets that serious little frown before saying 'Reeeally?'" Jen observed. Grudgingly, she added, "He does look way British and sort of cute."

Sam considered Ryan. "Looks aren't everything," she said as Linc Slocum guffawed at one of his own jokes. "Think of his bloodlines."

"He's a guy, not a horse, "Jen said, laughing. Her eyes glowed with thanks and she gave Sam's shoulder a gentle shove. "You are so good at cheering me up."

"Why do you need cheering up?" Sam asked.

"Some people just don't like weddings."

Sam's lips parted to ask why, but Jen's expression had changed. Her stare warned against it.

Sam felt chilled by Jen's look. Her best friend had been going through a tough time. Her parents were fighting. There was a chance they might leave Gold Dust Ranch, where Jen's dad was foreman, and move to town.

So Sam just smiled. She didn't want her best friend mad at her. Besides, if she was patient, Jen would explain.

But then Jen elbowed her. Hard.

"Ow! What was that for?" Sam gasped. She steadied her punch cup as it lapped near the edges. "You're just lucky I'm quick, because I really like this dress."

"Sorry," Jen said, but she didn't sound sincere. "You can forget watching Ryan," Jen said, pointing. "The real show is right over there."

Chapter Four

"Callie?" Sam asked.

"*Calliope* Thurston," Jen corrected. "A weird name for the weirdest kid in Nevada."

"She's not that weird. I was just talking with her." Sam watched the girl with the yellow hair and pierced nose move onto the dance floor.

"Don't you remember that day on the bus when everyone saw you with the Phantom and she implied you were a witch?"

"Sort of," Sam said. This probably wasn't the best time to bring up Callie's remark about communing with the stallion. Jen already sounded critical.

"How can you forget something like that?" Rachel Slocum stepped between Sam and Jen, inviting herself into their conversation.

Jen's index finger jabbed her glasses up her nose, while Sam shrugged.

"I was talking with her earlier," Sam repeated,

"and I kind of liked her."

Rachel fixed Sam with a disbelieving look. "Her parents are hippies."

Sam refocused on Callie. Before, she hadn't noticed the back of Callie's hair was shaved up her neck. Only the sides were long. And she did have that tiny gold stud in her nose and wore sixties-style clothes. That was unusual for this part of Nevada, but she wouldn't have attracted a single glance in San Francisco.

"They ran a health food store in Darton," Rachel confided, "until they got run out of town."

"By the Health Department or something?" Jen asked.

"How can it possibly matter?" Rachel asked, raising one plucked eyebrow.

Sam hoped Jen had heard the echo of her own nasty tone. But Sam's hope was crushed the next time Jen spoke.

"I wonder why you're sticking up for her?" Jen gave Sam a suspicious look.

"I'm not—"

"Did you know Callie's parents let her drop out of school?"

Callie was dancing with a guy Sam vaguely recognized. He was a hand from a local ranch, not a high school student.

Still, Callie had seemed smart while they were talking. She wasn't the type Sam imagined as a dropout. That did explain how she could be a hairdresser, though.

"She could've gotten sick and started failing classes," Sam mused. She'd fallen behind a few times, herself, because she was too busy with horses. "And she might have gotten discouraged, trying to catch up. I could see that, but I wonder why her parents let her quit?"

"Who knows why people like that do anything?" Rachel said, shuddering a little.

"It's true," Jen added. "She dropped out and, according to Clara from the café, she's living on her own in someone's converted garage. And she's only seventeen."

Jen sounded like a judgmental old woman, Sam thought.

No, wait. It was worse than that. She sounded like Rachel. Sam took a deep breath and bit her bottom lip to keep from saying so. If she wanted to end their friendship forever, all she'd have to do is tell Jen *that*.

Abruptly, Jen's focus shifted. Sam followed her glance to Jed and Lila Kenworthy. Jen's parents sat side by side on metal folding chairs. They held cups of punch and forced smiles onto their lips whenever anyone came up to chat, but they didn't talk to each other. The only thing they did together was watch the clock.

Sam noticed Jed's shoulder bump Lila's. Lila

drew her whole body away, as if she'd been burned.

No wonder Jen didn't like weddings.

As Rachel moved off to stand with her twin, Sam thought hard. There must be a way to improve Jen's mood. Before she came up with anything, Sam was interrupted.

"Excuse me, ladies," Dad said.

Sam looked up. How could Dad look familiar but foreign at the same time? His tanned cowboy face was kind and serious as always, but he stood straighter and taller. The black tuxedo coat and white shirt with little pleats down the front made him look like Dad, undercover.

"I know you're busy with your friends," Dad apologized. "But I was watching you from across the room and you look so pretty . . . I figured if I wanted to be the first to dance with you in a long fancy dress, I'd better quit wastin' time."

Dad swept the crowded reception hall with a glare.

"Guys aren't exactly waiting in line." Sam giggled.

"Only because I got here first," Dad told her.

He swept her into a dance. The slow, sweet song was something she almost recognized. At least her ears recognized it. Sam wasn't so sure about her feet.

Dad must have noticed her looking toward her high heels.

"You're doin' fine, honey," Dad said. "And you

look so grown up and lovely, I just . . ." Dad's voice trailed off.

He pressed his cheek to the top of her head. As Dad guided her in smooth steps, friends and relatives passed in a colorful whirl and Sam pressed her hand against Dad's back for balance. The crisp black cloth of the tuxedo jacket felt so different from Dad's flannel shirts.

"I'll be home before you know it," Dad said, but Sam heard a catch in his voice. The little bow he performed as he left her with Jen was so unlike Dad, Sam almost didn't notice how hard his jaw was set as he walked away.

Back toward Brynna, Sam thought a little sadly. But then she saw Brynna dab her eyes with a bride's lace handkerchief. And then Brynna blew Sam a kiss.

"She'll probably be good, as stepmothers go," Jen admitted. "At least she knows about horses."

Suddenly, Sam knew how to cheer Jen up again.

"Callie's adopting a mustang," Sam announced.

"Poor horse," Jen sneered. "She'll probably have it wearing crystals and love beads instead of a bridle."

Sam shifted her feet, listening to the rustle of her skirts. She was kind of mad at Jen for being so moody. In fact, she was about to give up on being the world's most determined best friend, when there was clapping and laughter from the other side of the room.

Sam stood on tiptoe, peering past the guests.

"They're cutting the cake!"

She didn't let Jen resist. She grabbed her friend's wrist and tugged her into a jog.

"Excuse me, Mrs. Allen." Sam smiled in regret as she passed Trudy Allen, who'd recently opened the Blind Faith Mustang Sanctuary. She should have stopped to talk, but this was her last chance at making Jen smile.

Sam towed Jen past friends and neighbors. Some said how nice she looked. But Sam kept moving, even when she sideswiped Jake's brother, who was six feet tall and solid as a cottonwood tree.

"Sorry, Brian," Sam apologized as she dragged a protesting Jen across the reception hall, then veered around two little kids and a lady carrying a tray full of dishes. Sam had no intention of slowing down.

Maybe if they were first in line, they'd get huge pieces of Gram's three-tiered, white-frosted fudge cake. If that didn't sweeten Jen's disposition, nothing would.

But Jen's attitude stayed sour until they hugged good-bye.

"Have fun in Utah," Sam said.

"I don't think that's possible," Jen answered. "But thanks for being a pal. I hope I didn't wreck your evening."

"Of course not," Sam assured her friend, but by the time Sam started for the parking lot and the serenity of Aunt Sue's minivan to go home, she was exhausted.

Aunt Sue was already in the driver's seat and the warning light from the open passenger's door made Sam walk a little faster, until she heard someone call her name.

"Samantha!"

Sam froze. The parking lot was pretty dark, but she didn't need to turn around to see who'd called.

Her hair might have dried, but her temper hadn't cooled, and that low voice could only belong to one person.

She wouldn't speak to *that person* even if he was the last human being on the face of the earth. If she were dying of thirst and he had the last cup of water, she wouldn't ask him for a sip. If she were drowning and he had the only life raft, she wouldn't shout "ahoy!"

Jake's boot steps crossed the asphalt parking lot. His hand touched her shoulder. Sam spun around with something like a growl rising in her throat.

"Don't bite my head off, Brat." He held both palms out as if warding off an attack. "I just want to talk."

"I'm not speaking to you."

"I have a question," Jake went on, as if he hadn't heard her. Then he waited for a response. When he didn't get one, he sighed. "Your hair got dirty . . ."

Jake hesitated and his cowboy bravado fell away.

His boots shifted in shy discomfort as he noticed Aunt Sue watching and eavesdropping from inside the van.

Like it or not, Sam knew she'd have to be a good listener if she wanted to understand what Jake had to say. Around strangers, he used sentences that were so short, they were like code.

Not that she felt sorry for him.

Sam crossed her arms at her waist, and let her head tilt to the side.

"You were just 'riding along minding your own business,' you said." Jake swallowed with such discomfort, Sam heard him.

But she didn't explain what had happened.

Let him suffer. She'd been willing to relate the details of the stampede before he'd doused her over the horse trough. If he thought she was torturing him now, he was wrong. She hadn't even started to pay him back.

Jake cracked his knuckles and watched his shiny black boot toe as it rearranged the parking lot gravel.

"D'you get thrown again?" he muttered.

"I got off"—Sam wanted to kick herself for speaking. Jake looked up quickly. She couldn't see his expression, but she'd bet he was looking all protective and brotherly—"in a hurry," she said.

"This have to do with that stud horse?" Jake's tone of voice warned that it had better not.

"Sam?" Aunt Sue called from inside the car. "I'm

ready to take off these high heels and have a cup of tea, honey. Can this wait?"

"Sure, Aunt Sue," Sam made her voice cheery, then added, "after all, it is Christmas Eve."

Jake didn't take the hint.

"Brynna told me about the mare," he said. "Don't be goin' out alone, looking for her."

Sam longed to imitate Jake's tough-guy tone and tell him she'd do whatever she pleased. Dad wouldn't be around to ride herd on her, and that meant freedom. There was no way she'd let Jake take Dad's place.

Wordless, Sam climbed into the minivan. As they drove away, she kept her eyes fixed on the rearview mirror. Jake still stood there alone and it looked like he was slamming his right fist into the palm of his left hand, over and over again.

It was only eight o'clock when they reached River Bend Ranch.

Little white holiday lights blinked around the windows on the two-story ranch house. The horses in the ten-acre pasture were dark shadows racing along the fence. Blaze, the Border collie, yapped six times as he stood on the front porch of the ranch house, keeping watch.

He must have been confused by the day's commotion, because usually he ran out to inspect strange vehicles. Or maybe Dallas, who'd left the reception early, had just given Blaze dinner and the dog was guarding his food dish.

The first thing Sam heard as she climbed out of the minivan was Ace. His lonely, melodic neigh floated overhead.

"Later, boy," Sam shouted toward the barn.

Aunt Sue's high heels crunched and her keys jingled as she came around the front of the van. "Does the horse know what you mean?" she asked.

"That was Ace," Sam said. "He's *my* horse and, well, even if he can't tell what 'later' means, he knows I heard him and returned his hello."

Sam leaned her head back and stared up at the night sky. Black and strewn with silver stars, it looked exactly the way a Christmas Eve sky should. There were only a few more nights left in a year that had been crowded with adventure. She'd moved from San Francisco to the ranch, and found Blackie, who'd turned from her long-lost colt into a wild white stallion with a band of his own. She'd battled wild horse rustlers, a disreputable rodeo contractor, and an orphaned cougar that thought she was lunch. . . .

Sam rolled her shoulders, vaguely aware that Aunt Sue had opened the back doors of her van. Sam was looking forward to a week of peace and quiet with Aunt Sue. She'd had enough excitement this year. And enough work.

This week, she wouldn't have to help Gram with the house and meals and Dad wouldn't be telling her to do more than her share of ranch chores.

"Two entire weeks without homework," Sam said with a sigh.

Aunt Sue chuckled. "I didn't bring mine, either. I have a stack of papers to grade at home, but they'll wait until I return home next week. I decided to make *this* week a real vacation."

"Do you need help carrying things?" Sam asked as Aunt Sue tugged her suitcase out of the back of the van.

"Actually, that nice man Dallas left the reception early so that he could bring most of it here for us."

"Great," Sam said, though she knew that Dallas had been uncomfortable about being part of the wedding from the beginning. He'd only dressed up and acted as Dad's best man because he saw it as a test of their friendship. He'd probably jumped at the chance to leave early.

"Can you make the dog step aside?" Aunt Sue asked as Blaze advanced on her, tail wagging.

"He's friendly," Sam assured her.

"I'm not afraid of him," Aunt Sue said. She placed her suitcase between herself and Blaze. "And I don't want to hurt his feelings, but he's a dirty dog and this red suit represents two weeks of my salary. Once I change into something more casual, I'll pet him so he knows I'm not the enemy."

Sam called Blaze away and considered Aunt Sue's attitude. Aunt Sue's only pets were a tank of well-behaved goldfish with long, silken fins. She treated all other animals like, well, animals.

Sam opened the door. Aunt Sue's presence made her newly aware of the smells of cinnamon, wood smoke, and the fresh pine scent of the Christmas tree. To her, the aromas meant home.

"The door wasn't locked."

Aunt Sue froze in the doorway, looking back into the dark ranch yard.

"We probably should lock it, but we don't," Sam said. "It's sort of a Western thing, I guess."

"A dangerous thing," Aunt Sue said. She whisked inside and locked the door behind them. "Out here all alone, without a neighbor in sight. You do have a telephone though, I see."

"And running water," Sam joked.

"I know you think I'm a hopeless city girl," Aunt Sue said, "but I have no desire to change. I'm going to leave all the ranch stuff to Dallas, just as your dad said, and spend my time spoiling you."

Sam tripped over her flounced hem as she hurried to hug Aunt Sue.

"You were so nice to give Dad and Brynna your apartment for their honeymoon," Sam said into her aunt's shoulder. "You're not even related to them, and well, Brynna — I mean — " Sam stopped. She'd had a rough time trying not to see Brynna as her mother's replacement.

Aunt Sue was Mom's sister, so how could she not feel the same?

"It's nothing," Aunt Sue said. She held Sam off at arm's length, but kept her hands on her shoulders. "I loved your mother. She loved Wyatt and I love you. It makes a perfect circle, and a great opportunity for us to spend some time together." Aunt Sue cleared her throat and rubbed her hands together in anticipation. "Now, what shall we do with the rest of our Christmas Eve?"

Chapter Five

Sam and Aunt Sue changed into cozy sweats and slippers.

Aunt Sue was staying in Gram's room for the week. As they met at the top of the stairs, they both realized they'd been too busy and excited to eat much at the wedding reception.

"I've decided calories don't exist this week," Aunt Sue said. "So, how does a mountain of popcorn sound? Covered with salt and butter, of course."

"Wonderful," Sam answered. "Bet I can beat you to the kitchen."

Fifteen minutes later, just as they settled on the living room couch with a big wooden bowl of popcorn, Cougar decided to introduce himself.

The brown-striped kitten suddenly appeared on the arm of the couch. He launched himself into Sam's lap and, instead of settling down, took one look at Aunt Sue, arched his back, and hissed.

At the same time, Blaze jumped to his feet. Eyes bleary with sleep, the Border collie shook his head and began barking.

"What in the world?" Aunt Sue swept the popcorn bowl out of reach of the kitten, but she needn't have bothered.

"Ow!" Sam yelped as Cougar dug in his tiny claws to steady himself before jumping toward the Christmas tree. "Oh no you don't!" she shouted, then jumped up and bolted after the kitten.

She must have sounded serious, because Cougar paused in his attempt to climb to the very top of the tree. Sam looked past the shiny ornaments to see Cougar clinging to the trunk, about halfway up. He met her eyes in a frustrated stare, gave a "pity me" mew, then skittered back down the trunk and vanished in the direction of the stairs.

"Blaze, stay," Sam ordered.

Walking stiff-legged, Blaze crossed to the rug in front of the fireplace. He turned around twice, then flung himself down. He gave a disgusted grunt, as if he couldn't believe Sam didn't want his help disciplining the fluffy juvenile delinquent.

"Do you think that's the end of the circus for the evening?" Aunt Sue placed the popcorn bowl back on the couch between them, but she still held the television's remote control.

"I'm pretty sure," Sam said.

After that, they ate each kernel of popcorn,

washed it down with cherry Cokes, and watched three cartoon Christmas specials Aunt Sue had copied onto videotape.

It was nearly midnight when Aunt Sue stretched and declared it was time for bed.

"Santa Claus won't come if you don't go nighty-night," she said, smiling.

Sam couldn't help glancing at the Christmas tree. She missed Dad already. She, Dad, and Brynna had agreed to open their presents after the honeymoon, but she noticed the mound of gifts had grown larger since this morning.

"You want to open one?" Aunt Sue asked.

"No, it's not that," Sam said.

She didn't want to be a demanding kid, but there was something she hadn't done in two years. She'd been looking forward to her first Christmas Eve back home, and even without Dad, she longed to resume one special tradition. Aunt Sue didn't have to go with her, if she didn't feel like it.

"We have this family custom," Sam said. "Have you ever heard the legend that animals can talk on Christmas Eve?"

"No, I can't say that I have. But it sounds like something an elementary school teacher like me should know," Aunt Sue said, encouraging Sam.

"The story goes that on the first Christmas, the baby was born in a barn and laid in a manger—I mean, we have mangers," Sam gestured toward the barn. "The horses eat out of them. And, anyway, all the animals knew something special had happened. Not just the cows and sheep and the donkey, but wild animals gathered at the barn door to gaze inside. They all kept watch over the baby. And for their"— Sam's hands spun in the air as she tried to think of the right word—"devotion, they were given the gift of being able to talk to the angels, one night each year."

"And tonight's the night," Aunt Sue said.

"Yeah," Sam said. "It's not that I really—"

"I think it sounds lovely," Aunt Sue said, cutting off Sam's excuses. "Did Louise do this with you when you were little?"

"Yes. And Dad and Gram, too," Sam said, but she couldn't manage to tell even Aunt Sue why the tradition was so important. Instead, she added, "We usually bring carrots for the horses."

"Lead the way," Aunt Sue said.

They turned off the porch light. No brightness shone through the bunkhouse windows, so Dallas must be asleep.

Together, Sam and Aunt Sue made their way across the ranch yard, lighting their way with candles. They'd have to blow out the flames before entering the barn, of course, but until then, they moved in small puddles of golden light.

As they were walking, a coyote howled. Aunt Sue gasped, but she didn't stop.

Starlight turned the sky silver-black and their

breaths hung like mist around them. The night felt magical.

"Do we sing?" Aunt Sue asked quietly.

"We could," Sam answered. "I think sometimes we did."

Aunt Sue began humming, "Away in a Manger."

"It seems appropriate," she said.

"Perfect," Sam managed a single word, but that was all. Her chest was full of some feeling that brought tears to her eyes.

The candle flame blurred before her, and all at once she thought about the Phantom. Once he'd lived in the warm barn. Sam remembered a Christmas Eve when he'd been a tiny black foal tucked next to his mother, a sorrel mustang named Princess Kitty. Now, he and his herd were on the cold range.

A strangely warm breeze swept across the ranch yard. It snuffed the candles and blew Sam's hair into her eyes. An owl hooted from the cottonwood tree in the big pasture. She knew the stallion would be safe and he'd take care of his mares and foals. She blinked away her worry and her tears as they walked inside the barn.

Straw rustled and big shapes moved at their approach. Sam clicked on the dim light in the tack room.

For a minute, it seemed there were only two colors in the barn: gold and dark charcoal gray. Sam breathed in the tang of saddle soap, the cereal smell of grain, and the sweet leathery scent of animals.

"That's Ace," Sam said, pointing out her horse. "And that's Sweetheart. She's an old girl," Sam said, as the pinto thrust her nose past Ace to sniff in Aunt Sue's direction. "She's Gram's horse, but Mom used to ride her." Sam's words caught in her throat for a minute, but Aunt Sue pretended not to notice.

"You don't have all the first Christmas animals at River Bend, do you?" she asked, peering around the barn.

"No sheep," Sam answered.

"I hear doves overhead in the rafters," Aunt Sue said, looking upward.

A cascade of chills ran down Sam's arms, but she tried not to remember why. And she didn't tell her aunt the birds in the rafters were just regular pigeons.

"Is that a cow?" Aunt Sue held her candle higher.

"That's Buddy," Sam said. "My baby Buddy."

Buddy was a leggy seven-month-old now, but she gave a calf-sized complaint about having her sleep disturbed. The sound was something between a moo and a bawl. Buddy shambled up to Sam and waited to have the pale hair between her ears rubbed. Sam massaged Buddy's poll. In thanks, the calf's long rough tongue licked Sam's cheek.

Refusing to be left out, Ace and Sweetheart crowded closer.

"Don't tell them they're filling in for donkeys," Sam whispered.

"Wouldn't think of it."

Ace lowered his head over the side of his stall until he was on eye level with Sam. His great brown eyes were glazed with faint light from the tack room, and he looked even more intelligent than usual.

His nostrils vibrated as he uttered a low nicker.

Was he reminding her he was a mustang? Was he promising to lead her to the red dun mare and help return the Phantom's herd to calm?

Sam couldn't tell.

"He really does look like he's about to talk," Aunt Sue said.

The little bay gelding who'd once run wild rubbed his forelock against Sam's shoulder. She slid her hand beneath his mane and along his neck. Ace bobbed his head in pleasure, pressing harder against her shoulder.

The cooing above sounded almost like language. In the quiet barn, Sam tried to understand the words.

"How should I tell him thank you?" Aunt Sue asked, pointing to Ace.

"For — ?"

"For making you happy."

"Just hold your hand flat," Sam said. "Let him sniff it, then pet his neck. He likes to be stroked under his mane."

Aunt Sue tried. She pulled the cuff of her lavender sweatshirt up as high as her elbow. She turned her hand over and extended it. She took a deep breath, then smiled as Ace's whiskers tickled her palm.

A feather floated down from the ceiling, spinning as it settled toward the straw. Sam looked upward, straining her eyes to see into the darkness. She saw nothing but a plump pigeon, making his way down a rafter.

Ace jerked his head up quick enough to startle both of them. Then he stamped, swished his tail, and swung his head back to look at Sweetheart.

"I could swear that animal looked disappointed," Aunt Sue said, as if she hadn't noticed the feather at all.

"He can smell the carrots," Sam said. "That's all."

She gave both horses their carrots, holding two in reserve.

"Want to give them the rest?"

Head tilted to one side, Aunt Sue stared with horrified fascination at Sweetheart's mouth.

"I think I'll pass," she said with forced calm. "Their teeth look like piano keys. Only wider and a good deal sharper."

"If you keep your thumb flat, they won't mistake it for a carrot," Sam instructed. "It's pretty fun."

"I wouldn't rob you of the pleasure," Aunt Sue said as Sam finished up and wiped her hands on her sweatpants. "Let's go back to the house and have a cup of cocoa to help us sleep."

Sam agreed.

"Good night everybody," she called to the animals as they left. To Aunt Sue, she added, "I guess this isn't the night they show us they can talk."

Blaze had waited outside the barn. Now, he rose and shook himself.

"They'll be at it once we're out of sight," Aunt Sue said, looking back over her shoulder. "Heaven only knows what they'll be saying about me."

The coyotes had moved their hunting far away and the owl in the cottonwood tree was quiet. Stillness spread around them like water.

Without the candles' light, it was very dark, but Aunt Sue went striding on ahead, thinking her own thoughts as she left Sam to follow.

In the silence, Sam could still hear the fluttering of wings in the rafters of the barn, and she let herself remember.

The first Christmas after her mother died, Dad had wanted to let their tradition lapse. Sam hadn't allowed it.

Thinking back, she could understand how hard it had been for Dad. Just the same, they'd walked across the dark barnyard. Only then, Dad and Gram had held the candles and she'd been in the middle, holding a hand from each of them.

She couldn't remember which horses had been there, but she remembered the smell of straw and apples. They must not have fed the horses carrots that year.

Overhead, she'd heard the rush and rustle of feathers.

The wings had belonged to pigeons, of course, but

the little kid she'd been had another idea.

Mama's angel.

Sam couldn't remember if she'd said anything aloud. She'd only been seven, but she might have kept it to herself. It hadn't taken her long to learn how easily questions about Mama could make her father sad.

Ever since then, she'd been certain such rustling was the sound of angel wings. Even now, Sam could picture her mother's pure white wings fluttering as she poised in the rafters, losing a feather some years, as she came back to Earth to look at the horses and check on her daughter at Christmas.

Sam stopped for a minute. She closed her eyes and listened with every cell in her body. A breeze picked its way through the few dry leaves remaining in the cottonwood tree. Sweetheart loosed a whinny of joyous recognition.

Then, midnight darkness wrapped around Sam, warm and gentle as a hug.

It's not my imagination, Sam thought. *It's just not.*

Chapter Six

Sam woke to a stack of presents and pizza for breakfast.

"You are so great!" Sam hugged Aunt Sue. "And I have no idea what to do first!" Sam's curiosity urged her to rip into the bright wrapping paper and see what was inside. Her stomach, however, growled at the aroma of ham and pineapple on a toasty pizza crust.

"How about both at once?" Aunt Sue urged. She disentangled herself from Sam's arms and brought a tray full of pizza and orange juice into the living room.

In the glow of the multicolored lights on the Christmas tree, Sam insisted Aunt Sue open her gifts first.

"I love it," Aunt Sue said, examining the red tote bag with a big apple on the side. A comical worm leaned out of the apple, holding a sign that said

Teachers Rock the World. "This will take the sting out of bringing home all those papers," Aunt Sue said.

"There's another one there from Dad and Gram," Sam said.

Though their present of Aunt Sue's favorite perfume was more costly, Sam could tell her aunt had liked her gift better.

Sam took her turn opening crossword puzzle books, the latest novels by her favorite authors, an incredible black sweater, and black jeans.

"It looks like you're out of your black phase," Aunt Sue said, fretting a little.

Sam shook her head. When she'd arrived at River Bend, she *had* been addicted to all black clothing. She didn't know why that changed, but it didn't matter.

"These are great!" Sam said. "I'm not saving them for two weeks 'til school starts up again, either."

"We'll think of an outing," Aunt Sue promised.

Sam had just opened her last two gifts—warm winter gloves and a huge picture book of Friesian horses—when she heard Buddy's moo.

"Oh my gosh! How could I have forgotten!" Sam stood suddenly, scattering wrapping paper and boxes. "The animals need to be fed. I should have taken care of them first."

"Relax," Aunt Sue told her. "Your foreman Dallas told me he'd take care of the animals before he left this morning."

"Left?" Sam felt a second surge of guilt. Why hadn't

she thought of Dallas spending Christmas alone?

"Yesterday at the wedding, he told me he'd be gone for the day," Aunt Sue said. "A gathering of 'misfits,' he said, was having Christmas breakfast at Clara's Diner, then watching football all day. He didn't sound a bit sorry for himself, Sam. It was easy to see he much preferred that get-together over brunch and dinner with us—although I invited him, of course—so relax."

Sam settled back onto the floor. Sitting cross-legged, she played chase-the-ribbon with Cougar until Dad and Brynna called.

They loved Aunt Sue's apartment. The city view and fog pressing against the wide bay windows were so different from Nevada. Sam told Dad about her new book, filled with tall black horses with flowing manes and tails and didn't feel a twinge of jealousy. When she hung up, she felt satisfied and warm.

It was the start of a great day. Sam and Aunt Sue worked together on crossword puzzles while the radio played carols, hymns, and oldies and Aunt Sue sang along. She got an early start on dinner, assembling a pasta, cheese, and crabmeat casserole that was Sam's favorite.

Sam did nothing more energetic than dressing in faded jeans and an old red flannel shirt. Then, she read one of her new books with Cougar curled up, purring on her tummy.

The paperback mystery had her locked in its spell

when the phone rang. It was Jen.

Sam was so happy to hear from her friend once more before she left for Utah, she tried to brush aside Jen's apology.

"I don't know why I was in such a toxic mood, but I shouldn't have let it spill over on you. Say you forgive me," Jen pleaded.

"Like you've never put up with one of my bad moods," Sam said. "Of course I forgive you."

"Know how I shook it off?" Jen asked in a whisper. "I woke up at about four A.M. and worked under the covers with a flashlight on some calculus that Mr. Wilson gave me for extra credit. That always cheers me up, but I don't think Mom and Dad would think it was appropriate for the holiday."

"You are so smart, it's creepy," Sam said.

Jen laughed and promised that if she returned home in time, they'd go riding. Sam agreed, then headed back to the couch and stayed there, reading, feeling loose and lazy.

I like being pampered, Sam was thinking, when suddenly she became aware that she hadn't heard any utensils clanging or water running, or any sound at all from the kitchen for a while.

"Aunt Sue?" she called. When there was no answer, Sam went to investigate.

Aunt Sue stood at the big window that looked across the ranch yard and bridge toward the snow-capped Calico Mountains. At first Sam thought her aunt was merely admiring the view. As she moved closer, though, Sam saw the mustangs.

"Aren't they great," Sam sighed. She stood beside her aunt. When she didn't answer, Sam glanced sideways.

"They are interesting," Aunt Sue managed, but she wore a tight-lipped expression.

Sam felt a fizz of warning throughout her body. Aunt Sue might have been looking at a mass of deadly poisonous snakes instead of horses.

"I'm going to walk out on the bridge and watch them a while," Sam said. "Do you want to come?"

Aunt Sue shook her head. "Are you allowed to go out there?" she asked.

"I'm allowed to go almost anywhere within a day's ride of the ranch, as long as I tell someone where I'm going," Sam said. Aunt Sue was trusting her to tell the truth and she had. Sam saw no reason to mention she'd broken that rule a time or two.

"You'll just go out on the bridge?" Aunt Sue verified, as Sam fidgeted by the door.

"They'll probably be gone by the time I get there," Sam said. "Just watch. Once they hear the door open, they'll take off."

"Like deer," Aunt Sue said, nodding.

"Just like deer," Sam said, but she really didn't know how the mustangs would react. Being this close to the ranch in broad daylight was unusual behavior. She half believed they'd come to remind her of her promise to find their missing lead mare.

Sam didn't take time to go back upstairs and get her boots. Her sneakers would have to do. She grabbed her leather jacket from the porch hook, gave her worried aunt a wave, and slipped outside. If she dawdled, the horses would be gone.

A cold wind blasted in Sam's face as she came out onto the porch. She pulled her jacket closer and hurried.

The mustangs were short-tempered, snorting and lashing out with their heels as Sam approached the bridge. By the time she was halfway across the wooden bridge, the mares had backed away from the shore on the wild side of the river.

They didn't move fast enough to suit the Phantom.

The stallion charged down from the hillside, scattering the mares in his path. Although she was at least a quarter-mile away, with the river between them, the Phantom warned her with flattened ears and flashing teeth.

"It's okay, boy," Sam said, puzzled.

He knew her. He couldn't believe she'd harm his band. Still, he wasn't acting like her horse.

From this distance, she wouldn't risk calling out the secret name that would remind him of their bond. She was pretty sure it wouldn't matter if she did.

Now, he wasn't Zanzibar. He was all wild stallion. Under the dull winter sky, he looked gray and shaggy. There was a weariness in the way he trotted up the riverbank, tossing his head. His thick muscles bunched and worked under his hide. He was built for strength and fleetness, but the silver iridescence that usually danced on his coat just wasn't there.

He didn't look sick. He looked tired.

"I'm so glad there are no challengers around," Sam muttered.

She scanned the mountains. Except for sagebrush and piñon pines swaying in the wind, nothing moved. Her eyes searched the range in every direction and she kept her fingers crossed.

Just weeks ago, the Phantom's son had challenged him. She'd seen a young chestnut named Yellowtail, too, who was eager to add to his small family of mares.

She wouldn't expect to see another stallion at this time of year, but that didn't mean the Phantom was safe. His herd was larger than most mustang bands. He needed the red dun if he was going to keep it.

As if he'd heard her thoughts, the stallion ran a circle around his mares, then he stopped and pawed. He uttered guttural orders that sounded like, *git, git,* then lowered his head. His mane rushed forward and his muzzle nearly reached the ground as he snaked his head in a herding motion.

The mares fled, some straying right, until the Phantom darted after them. And then they were gone.

When Sam walked back into the house, her wind-scoured cheeks felt hot. Aunt Sue was preheating the oven for the casserole and the kitchen was warm. She'd just shrugged out of her coat when she realized Aunt Sue was holding binoculars.

Sam made herself look away. She didn't ask where they'd come from or why Aunt Sue was spying on her, but she didn't like it.

Sam faced the coatrack. Taking longer than she needed to, she hung her jacket and gave herself some good advice. *Let it go.*

"While I'm here, I think you should stay away from those wild horses."

Sam turned in time to see Aunt Sue return to the counter where she'd been working on the casserole.

It was Christmas Day. Sam didn't want to fight, but she didn't need to be watched like a little kid, either.

"I really wanted to bring fresh crab for this," Aunt Sue said, crimping a piece of aluminum foil over the dish. "But fresh crabs don't travel very well, so I had to use canned."

Staring at her aunt's back, Sam guessed they were both trying to do the same thing—avoid conflict.

Sam's mature half told her again: let it go. The Phantom wasn't going to be coming to her this week, anyhow. That other half of her couldn't resist speaking just one sentence.

"Aunt Sue, they're only horses."

Aunt Sue turned slowly with the covered casserole in her hands.

"Horses are unpredictable. They're strong and scared of the slightest little thing and they have no more sense of right and wrong than—" Aunt Sue set the casserole down on the counter and slapped one hand against the white refrigerator "—than *this*. And they weigh just as much."

Sam tried to be patient, but Aunt Sue was showing her ignorance. Living in the city didn't excuse this kind of mistake.

"A horse," Sam said slowly, "is smarter than a refrigerator."

"Oh, really? Then why would the horse you raised from a baby try to kill you?"

Sam gasped. Why hadn't she guessed what Aunt Sue was thinking?

"Blackie didn't try to kill me," Sam protested.

Aunt Sue didn't seem to hear. She stared straight ahead as if that day were replaying on an invisible movie screen.

"I was teaching summer school when your Gram called and told me you'd been brought in from one of the outlying pastures, unconscious. I took a cab to the San Francisco airport and caught the first flight out to Reno, where I paid another cab to break the speed limit as we drove over miles of dark desert. When I arrived at the hospital I had no idea if you'd be alive. Thank God, you were."

Sam was sorry she'd ever opened her mouth. She didn't want Aunt Sue to live through this again. Why hadn't she taken her own advice and just kept quiet? She held out her hands in a calming motion.

"I'm sorry. I forgot. We don't have to talk about this."

"I think we do," Aunt Sue said.

Sam smothered a moan as Aunt Sue pulled two chairs out from the table.

"You opened this can of worms, Samantha. You're old enough to see what's inside."

Sam sat, but she felt so suddenly sick to her stomach, she really thought she might vomit. She tried to push back the fear that had clamped her just yesterday when she'd fallen. More than anything, she wanted to forget about the accident that had happened nearly two and a half years ago.

"Your father and Grace were sitting in the waiting room. Grace got up and told me what she could, but your father just sat there. His hands hung loose between his knees and he looked down toward his boots. I really don't think he knew I was there and I'm sure he didn't hear Grace telling me about your fractured skull and your chances for survival."

Sam took a deep breath. Why couldn't she have heard this some other time, when she wasn't feeling timid about galloping? She couldn't come up with a single argument to throw back at Aunt Sue.

"When Wyatt finally looked up, his face was a

terrible thing to see." Aunt Sue rubbed her arms as if she felt a chill. "He left the waiting room. We heard him dropping coins into a pay phone down the hall and there was no doubt in my mind he was calling to have someone hunt that horse down and kill it."

The kitchen lay quiet around them. Sam heard the fireplace crackling in the other room and the wind shaking the trees outside. Then, she heard an inquiring mew and clicks of excited clawing.

"Cougar, no!" Sam jumped up and grabbed her kitten. If he'd been a little taller, he might have reached the crab casserole on the counter.

"That's finished," Aunt Sue said.

Sam wasn't sure whether she meant the casserole or the day of the accident, but Aunt Sue rose from the table and whisked the casserole into the oven.

Sam draped Cougar over her shoulder, facing him away from the food. She petted his back rapidly, hoping to distract him.

"Settle down, Cougar. Come on," Sam crooned. When he finally started purring, she was glad. This wasn't a good time for Cougar to experiment with catching his own dinner.

Aunt Sue stood staring at the stove. There was nothing to look at, but she stared just the same.

Suddenly, Sam thought of Jake. Since the accident, he'd been torn with guilt. Yes, he'd rushed her through a gate on a green horse and, as she fell, Blackie's hoof had struck her head. But Jake was the one who'd gone for help. He was responsible for saving her life, but he didn't see it that way.

"Was Jake there at the hospital?" Sam asked.

"Not that first night. It was only the three of us, waiting. You were out of surgery, but no one had been allowed to see you."

"But . . . ?" Sam closed her lips.

Discussing Jake's concern with Aunt Sue would increase the chance they'd get together and decide she wasn't allowed to ride any mount more challenging than a pony on a lead rein.

Aunt Sue met Sam's eyes, clearly waiting for her to finish the question.

No way. Sam jiggled Cougar on her shoulder as he started to get restless. Distraction had worked with the kitten. She might as well try it on Aunt Sue.

"About Jake," Sam said. "He would've taken me up to Willow Springs Wild Horse Center tomorrow, but he's busy."

That wasn't a lie. Jake's dad wanted his seven sons to dig up and repair the Three Ponies Ranch irrigation system during their break from school.

"Is it completely out of the question," Sam asked, "that you'd, you know, drive me up there tomorrow?"

Aunt Sue didn't pin her down. She didn't inquire why Sam wanted to go, but she did ask, "Are they in cages?"

Since it wasn't a good time to laugh, Sam said, "In corrals, yes."

"Okay, I'll do it. I'm here to spoil you, after all. In addition, I don't trust another soul to watch you like I will. Don't look so relieved. If you touch a pinky to a wild horse, that's it. You'll sit in this house and watch Disney videos until your father gets home. Understood?"

"Absolutely," Sam said, and because she couldn't suppress her sigh of relief, she followed it with an offer. "Can I help you with dinner?"

"No, you can't. Go take a bubble bath or something."

Sam turned toward the stairs, thinking she might just do that when Aunt Sue called after her.

"Sam?" Aunt Sue stood with her feet braced apart and her hands on her hips. "I've only got one niece, honey, and I plan to take care of her."

Chapter Seven

Wind had swept the skies clear of all but the highest, wispiest clouds.

"A perfect blue-and-white day," Aunt Sue said as she locked the front door and looked into the skies. "Aren't those clouds called 'mares' tails'?"

"I hope so," Sam said. She was thinking that would bode well for finding the tiger dun, but Aunt Sue didn't seem to understand.

Sam felt a little disoriented. Last night she'd dreamed of falling. She'd stumbled off the Golden Gate Bridge and ended up plummeting toward Arroyo Azul.

Weird, she thought, but it didn't take long for the December weather to sweep her nightmare aside.

With each breath, the cold wind raced through her nose, down into her lungs and Sam was glad she'd snagged her jacket. She wore her favorite russet sweater with her new black jeans, but they were no match for the piercing wind.

Aunt Sue wore trim khaki pants with a turtleneck and blazer. Country casual, San Francisco style, Sam thought.

As they drove down the highway toward Willow Springs, Aunt Sue commented on the limitless vistas and sage-dotted spaciousness of the range. Sam knew her aunt was just filling the moments, hoping Sam would suddenly confess what she wanted to do at the wild horse corrals. That was one big difference between Aunt Sue and Gram. Aunt Sue was so patient.

"The horse I'm hoping to find up here," Sam began, "is the lead mare of the herd you saw yesterday."

Aunt Sue's fingers tightened on the steering wheel before she said, "They have a female boss? Not that white stallion?"

"They sort of share the leadership," Sam explained. "And when she's missing, he can't really handle a herd that big."

"Why go looking for her? Won't she just come back on her own after she's had her vacation?"

"Wild horses aren't like people," Sam said. "The herd is everything to them. It's not just a family, but their home and a shield against danger. They all watch out for each other and they don't leave unless they're driven out—which the Phantom wouldn't do to her—or unless they're hurt and get left behind."

"They leave their injured behind?" Aunt Sue said, frowning.

"Sometimes," Sam admitted, though she didn't want Aunt Sue to think badly of the horses. "Everybody tells me it's for the good of the herd. An injured horse attracts predators and then if something like a cougar or a pack of coyotes comes by and sees the foals, they'd go after them instead."

Aunt Sue followed Sam's gesture to turn right at the sign for Willow Springs.

"After this, the road just keeps climbing. There's a narrow part called Thread the Needle. Then it drops into a valley full of BLM corrals and an office," Sam explained.

"Piece of cake," Aunt Sue said, then added, "and what if this lead mare is up here?"

For a minute, that question stopped Sam. She'd promised to get the mare back to her herd, but she didn't really have a plan.

"If she's there, I'll find out why. Brynna said there weren't any gathers planned, so she didn't think the mare would be there. But if she is, I'll tell Brynna and she'll help me figure some way for the mare to rejoin her band."

Sam noticed Aunt Sue's inquiring look, but she didn't try to interpret it. She was more worried about Mr. Norman White, Brynna's substitute. She knew for a fact that Mr. White had no qualms about destroying horses.

The van made a chugging sound as Aunt Sue downshifted.

"This would be a tricky bit of road if you weren't expecting it," she said as the road narrowed to barely accommodate the van. Aunt Sue drove on a bit, glanced to her left at a sidehill slanting like a slide into a maze of deer trails. "Looking at that too long could give a person vertigo. You know, that dizzy feeling of falling forward?"

"I know," Sam said. "Gram doesn't like this place, either. And to tell the truth, when I get my license . . ."

"Don't worry about it," Aunt Sue dismissed Sam's anxiety. "The trick is to let your eyes rest where you want the car to go. That definitely wouldn't call for peeking over the edge."

For the first time, Sam thought she might turn out to be a good driver.

"That's what you do when you're riding, too," Sam said.

"Really?" Aunt Sue shot a quick glance Sam's way. "If that smirk is because you think you can get me up on some equine monster, you can just forget about it."

"Yes, ma'am," Sam said, but the idea made her grin.

Even though Aunt Sue wasn't an experienced mountain driver, she had more confidence than people who'd lived here all their lives.

Once, when she'd driven up here with Mrs. Allen, owner of Deerpath Ranch and the new wild horse sanctuary, Sam was sure she'd seen the older lady jab her foot on the accelerator and close her eyes, just to get past this narrow spot.

Just past the summit, the road dipped down toward dozens of corrals filled with hundreds of horses. A few horses fled the approach of the mini-van, running to the other side of their enclosure, and kept their heads turned toward the new vehicle, but none of them looked very scared.

Aunt Sue angled the van toward a small patch of asphalt where two white off-road vehicles belonging to BLM were parked near a rental truck with a huge horse trailer coupled on behind.

Could Callie be taking her adopted mustang home today?

As they climbed out of the van, Aunt Sue rubbed her hands up and down her blazer sleeves. The drop in temperature underlined the increase in altitude.

As they walked toward the BLM office, Sam recognized Norman White. Dressed in a crisp tan uniform, he had a stiff little mustache that twitched as he talked to Callie Thurston.

Since they were still yards away, Sam couldn't tell what he was saying, but Mr. White was gesturing with a folder. Each time the wind gusted, he stepped back.

Callie wore a moss-green cloak that swirled around her and threatened to wrap Mr. White in its folds as well. Sam knew the garment would frighten a horse fresh off the range, but Mr. White wasn't a horse.

As they drew closer, Sam thought he looked tense and muscular in a self-conscious way. His short hair stuck up like the bristles of her toothbrush. And there he went, hopping out of the way of the cloak, again. Mr. White was trying so hard not to look silly, that he did.

He also broke off his conversation with Callie as he noticed her. He didn't greet her like an acquaintance, didn't mention Brynna had talked with him about the lead mare, or even needle her about coming to rescue more unadoptable horses. He gave a curt nod and kept talking.

Fine, Sam thought. She'd begin a search for the tiger dun mare, until Mr. White made time for her.

Aunt Sue followed Sam over to one of the pens. Through the fence rails, they saw about a dozen horses.

"That blond one's nice looking," Aunt Sue said.

Sam smiled. At least Aunt Sue was trying to show some interest in horses.

"That's a palomino," Sam explained gently. "My friend Jen rides one."

Sam kept looking for the tiger dun, but most of the mustangs were bays and chestnuts. A single Appaloosa with blue roan splatters stood apart from the others.

"They're all young horses, yearlings or so. She wouldn't be with them," Sam confided to Aunt Sue. "That's the corral I want to check."

Sam nodded toward the pen closest to Callie. One end of the enclosure had a squeeze chute, which would keep a horse confined so that it could be inoculated or given vitamins. It also had a ramp that would make loading a horse into a trailer easier. Sam sensed movement inside the corral, but she couldn't see the horse.

It had to be the mustang Callie was adopting, so the horse wouldn't be here when Brynna returned. If it *was* the red dun mare, that meant trouble.

". . . your parents?"

Wind caught most of Mr. White's question, but Sam heard Callie's answer.

"If you'll check my application, you'll see they've already signed it. Plus, I'm an emancipated minor, so I can do this on my own."

Sam turned to Aunt Sue, whispering, "What exactly is an 'emancipated minor'?"

At first, Sam wasn't sure Aunt Sue had heard her question.

"That's the girl from the beauty college, isn't it? The one who did such miracles with our hair." Aunt Sue studied Callie for a few seconds. "It means she's under eighteen years old and her parents have legally freed her from their control."

"Why would they do that?" Sam asked, but Aunt Sue was motioning her to silence.

". . . corral must be four hundred feet square with tall, strong fences. A round pen is ideal for breaking her to halter and for the approach and retreat training method BLM suggests for wild horses." Mr. White's mustache twitched as if he thought the technique was nonsense. Sam would bet he was an advocate of showing horses who was boss, rather than working with their natural instincts.

"She doesn't have it," Aunt Sue muttered.

"Have what?" Sam noticed Aunt Sue was watching Callie, not Mr. White, and Callie definitely looked uneasy.

Mr. White was going on about training and shelter, while Callie twisted her fingers in a fold of her cloak and gave slow, halting nods.

"An official from BLM or a humane organization will come out and inspect the facility and verify your horse's health. I'll supply you with a card that must be kept up-to-date and produced on demand. The freeze brand tells the animal's estimated year of birth, where she was gathered . . ."

Callie fidgeted with a pendant that hung around her neck amid a layer of other necklaces. And she chewed her lower lip.

". . . belongs to the United States government and if she dies, escapes, or is stolen you must report—"

"I know about gaining title to her," Callie said. "But what about her feet?"

Her feet? If there was something wrong with the mare's hooves, Callie needed to be quiet.

No hooves, no horse. That's what Dallas always said.

If Mr. White agreed, he might want to put her down.

"She has a cracked hoof," Callie explained. "That's why she was brought in."

Sam moved closer. A cracked hoof. That might make the mare temporarily lame, or it could cripple her. Either way, the condition would slow a horse down. She might be left behind and gathered by a BLM wrangler.

Sam strode away from Aunt Sue. It might seem like she was intruding on Callie's conversation, but she had to see the horse they were talking about. Sam peered between two fence rails at the horse inside.

The mare stood straight and slim as a Thoroughbred. Her slender legs wore horizontal bars of black, and a dark stripe traced the path of her spine. Her black-edged ears pricked to listen and her slightly dished head turned toward Sam. The horse trembled with watchfulness.

"Oh girl," Sam said with a sigh.

The mare was the color of autumn leaves, of fiery sunsets, of every beautiful red thing in nature. The Phantom's red dun lead mare was a prisoner.

She didn't belong in this pen. She couldn't belong to Callie Thurston.

Sam squared her shoulders and lifted her chin. She was the only one who cared about returning the mare to her herd, so she'd better get started with that rescue, right now.

Chapter Eight

"Sam!" Callie's voice soared with delight. "I knew Queen and I were meant to be together!" She clapped her hands and laughed.

"Huh?"

It wasn't the most intelligent response to Callie's greeting, but Sam didn't know what in the world Callie was talking about.

"From the moment my eyes met Queen's, there was a connection, a bond," Callie said. Her hands cupped around her pendant, as if warming it. "When a problem came up this morning, logic told me to cancel the adoption. But I'd already rented the horse trailer and even though I had no place to take her, some sixth sense told me a way would be provided. And here you are!"

A way would be provided. The phrase sounded other-worldly, as if Callie had expected something paranormal to happen. If that was the case, Sam knew she didn't fit that description.

Sam looked to Aunt Sue for help. Because she'd been a teacher for so long, she was usually pretty good at reading kids, but Aunt Sue's frown showed she was equally puzzled. Sam looked at Mr. White. Tapping the file folder against his palm, he stared at Callie as if she spoke another language.

Sam's mind spun. Queen had to be the red dun. It was a fitting name for a lead mare, so maybe Callie did have some sort of intuition. But how did Callie suppose normal, everyday, Sam Forster fit into this mystical match?

"Just why do you think I'm that 'way'?" Sam asked, embarrassed.

"I'd been depending on a friend to supply a corral for Queen, but that didn't work out," Callie began to explain.

"Let me see if I understand you correctly," Mr. White interrupted. "You don't have the proper facilities for a healthy animal, let alone an injured one?"

Sam's heart bumped into high speed. This was just what she'd feared.

Mr. White was focusing on the mare's injury. Who knew what twisted solution he'd reach?

"Wouldn't an injury make her even easier to confine?" Aunt Sue spoke up. "I'm no horse expert, but I've had sore feet from wearing high heels. At the end of the day, I don't exactly feel like running across the prairie."

"Pardon me?" Mr. White said and Sam was pretty sure he wanted to ask Aunt Sue who the heck she was, but things were getting so weird, he didn't know where to start.

Sam didn't know whether to thank Aunt Sue or tell her to hush.

The mare belonged on the range.

If the adoption was finalized, Callie couldn't turn her loose, even if Sam convinced her it was the right thing to do.

If the mare was kept here at Willow Springs, her future was uncertain.

If the mare's hoof was badly damaged, she would be easy prey for a predator.

Aunt Sue took pity on Norman White's confusion. She stepped forward with her hand extended.

"Hi. I'm Samantha's aunt. I guess that sort of makes me Brynna Olson—oops—Brynna *Forster*'s sister-in-law. Almost." Aunt Sue shook Mr. White's unresisting hand. "I certainly didn't mean to barge into your conversation. Actually, it's the first time I've seen so many horses. I've encountered a few in Golden Gate Park, when I jog."

Aunt Sue flashed Sam a glance that said she was doing her best to stall. But Sam didn't know what to do next.

She needed the truth about the mare's hoof. Would it heal? How well?

There was a big difference between captivity and

the wild. A caring rider could tend a hoof and keep a horse on good footing. Once she was free, the mare would lead her band where food and water were plentiful, regardless of the conditions.

Sam had ridden in mustang country and she knew the wild horses crossed ground that was dangerous. She'd ridden the hard-baked playa and stretches of terrain littered with sharp black volcanic rock. She'd traversed shale layered on a hillside like china plates and been scared silly. One misstep in a place like that could send a horse sliding to its death.

The images flashed through her mind in an instant, making things even more complicated. Sam scanned the acres of wild horses and hay bales, looking for help. She found it when she spotted a big man with a full black beard.

The first day she'd seen him, he'd been throwing hay to the corralled horses and she'd nicknamed him Bale-Tosser in her mind. The last time Mr. White had substituted for Brynna, Bale-Tosser had helped block the destruction of the group of mustangs Mr. White called "unadoptable."

Now, he walked toward Sam and gave her a quick wink. He looked like a buckaroo, not a bureaucrat.

"Ready to load the princess?" he asked.

"Queen," Callie corrected. "Not Princess."

"All I know's she acts like royalty. Scared and hurtin' like she was, she still tried to boss around those other mares we put her in with."

"Adoption may not be an option, if she's badly injured," Mr. White said.

"Shoot, we have special adoptions all the time," Bale-Tosser said. His tone was easy, not like he was correcting Mr. White, just telling him about the normal events at Willow Springs Wild Horse Center. "Some horses have accidents that render 'em blind, for instance. And, long as they have some other horse to guide on, they do fine in the wild. In pastures, too, for that matter."

"Yes, but—"

"Just last month we had that beautiful little filly with the twisted legs and she got adopted."

Sam recognized the description of a flaxen-maned filly that Mrs. Allen had rescued along with twelve other horses before Mr. White could have them destroyed. By the twitch of his mustache, Mr. White clearly didn't appreciate the reminder.

"What is the prognosis on this animal?" he snapped.

"She's doin' okay. Dr. Scott, that's our veterinar- ian—"

"Oh, I recall Dr. Scott," Mr. White said.

"—says, she'll need expert farrier care soon as Silas Lake can touch her feet." Bale-Tosser paused to reach for the folder Mr. White was holding. "Mind if I see that?"

In the seconds Mr. White hesitated, Sam

remembered Silas Lake. Though Dad and Dallas did the shoeing for River Bend's horses, Mrs. Allen had used Silas Lake for hers.

That was no simple chore, especially when it came to Calico. Mrs. Allen treated her big paint mare like a pet, but the farrier had left swearing that the horse was a naturally born carnivore.

"Thanks," Bale-Tosser said as Mr. White surrendered the folder. "Yeah, see right here?" Bale-Tosser tapped a note clipped inside the folder. "Dr. Scott recommended Silas by name."

Mr. White looked toward the horizon, but Sam could see in his eyes that he thought Dr. Scott was too soft. Sam had heard him say those very words to the blond, bespectacled vet when he refused to put down a blind foal.

For that and his gentle, expert handling of the Phantom in the rodeo arena, Dr. Scott was Sam's hero.

"Are you willing to give Queen lots of extra handling, sorta speed up the gentling process so Silas can take care of those hooves?" Bale-Tosser asked Callie.

"Of course," Callie said. "I'd keep her in my bedroom if I could."

"Which brings us back to the problem at hand," said Mr. White. He leaned toward Callie in a way that was supposed to look friendly. "You don't know where you'll keep her."

"I've taken every extra job I can," Callie said,

flashing a thankful smile at Aunt Sue. "And I've been living on noodles so that I could buy all the right food for Queen, but I was hoping . . ."

Don't say it, Sam begged silently.

". . . maybe . . ."

Please don't say it.

"Queen could stay at River Bend Ranch until I get my own place."

An icy gust of wind cooled Sam's forehead and she realized she was sweating.

What's the big deal? she asked herself. The only promise she'd made had been to a horse.

But she loved that horse.

If the Phantom had no lead mare by spring, he'd be beset by other stallions trying to steal his band. Doing battle, he could be hurt. He could be killed.

A small plane passed overhead. As it did, the red dun bolted, stumbling as her sore hoof hit the ground. Just before she collided with a fence, she swung around and ran back in the opposite direction.

It was then Sam saw the white freeze brand on her neck.

Of course. Why hadn't she realized this before?

The mare wouldn't be released. That brand meant she was now the property of the United States government. The only question was whether she'd be adopted by Callie Thurston or someone else.

Better Callie, Sam decided.

If she waited for another adopter, she'd have to

stay at Willow Springs, under Mr. White's supervision during the week Brynna was gone.

Sam didn't trust Mr. White. She wanted to get the mare out of his reach.

"Ma'am?" Bale-Tosser turned to Aunt Sue.

Sam guessed it was only fair. Aunt Sue was the adult in charge, even if she didn't know a palomino from a blond.

Aunt Sue put the fingers of both hands together, then flexed her knuckles. The gesture reminded Sam of a spider doing push-ups on a mirror, but she knew from the time they'd lived together, this meant Aunt Sue was thinking. Hard.

"Samantha?" Aunt Sue asked.

"We just finished a round pen to BLM specifications, and we're already cleared as adopters because of the HARP horses," Sam said.

The echo of her own voice sounded as official and cold as Mr. White's, but she didn't want to get excited about Queen. After all, they were stealing her from the Phantom.

"Very well," Aunt Sue said in her teacher voice. "I agree, if she's kept locked in her cage until Brynna gets home. And no one goes into that—all right," she put in, remembering Sam's earlier correction, "—*pen*, with her."

Sam's eyes met Callie's. They both knew Queen needed human contact to start forming a new herd, a family that included humans. Isolating her was the last thing they should do.

Sam shrugged and gestured toward Callie.

All at once Sam felt really irritated by Callie's constant fiddling with her necklace, and her pierced nose and her Dracula cloak.

This wasn't what Sam had planned. Not even close. She wanted to fling the gate wide, make a whoop so loud people would think it was a fire engine, and watch the red dun mare run. Sam wanted to see her gallop through Thread the Needle, down the hill. She wanted to see her splash through the shallows of La Charla, and emerge on the wild side of the river.

The red dun mare ran a lap around her corral in a lopsided gait, then stopped. She held one hoof clear of the dirt. She shook her mane and nearly fell. Then, she uttered a long, sad neigh in the direction of the Calico Mountains.

How awful if she can read my mind, Sam thought.

How awful if she knows she'll never be free again. Ever.

Chapter Nine

It took three men and two hours to load the red dun into the trailer.

Sam had known the delicate, doelike mustang would fight confinement, but she hadn't guessed the battle would be so sad.

When escape proved impossible, the mare squealed in fury, trying to back down the men she saw as tormenters. When that didn't work, she used her strength against them. The men were patient, working with her instincts instead of forcing her, but the mare stood firm.

Once the plunging mare was loaded, they gave her no chance to back out. The trailer door was latched behind her when she snagged the cheek piece of her new black halter and began jerking back and scrambling to stay upright.

"Aw, shoot," Bale-Tosser moaned as the mare's neck wrenched at an unnatural angle.

Instantly, he clambered over the chute fence, leaned against the trailer, and his arm darted out, trying to release the metal slide that held the halter in place.

The commotion was brief. He fell back to the ground, stood, and stamped the dust from his boots.

"Worked just like it was supposed to," he said. He examined the bones in the back of his hand and gently flexed his fingers. "Instead of fussing with knots and buckles, the thing fell right off."

"I can take her without a halter," Callie offered.

"No you can't," Bale-Tosser insisted. "She leaves here with a halter and that ten-foot lead rope you brought."

Sam sighed. Haltering the mare had taken forever. She must have thought they were predators, going for her vulnerable eyes.

Now they'd have to do it again.

Bale-Tosser read Sam's expression and shook his head. "Lots more fun to get it on her again than get your fingers outta a knot that has hundreds of pounds of horse jerking it tighter and tighter. Fingers can be sorta useful to those of us workin' with mustangs."

For a few minutes, Willow Springs was silent, except for the breathing of the tired horse and confounded men.

The mare faced away from them, but she made the mouthing movements of a foal.

Sam knew the red dun was promising the men could rule her, if only they'd leave her alone.

"Let's take a coffee break before we try haltering her again. It will give her a chance to get used to her surroundings," said Bale-Tosser, glancing at his hand again. "I can get some ice on this."

Everyone nodded. Mr. White, of course, had long since returned to his warm office. The perfect blue-and-white day had turned gray. Sam hoped it wouldn't rain.

Hooves thudded inside the trailer as the mare looked for a way out.

Now Sam realized why the BLM required a big horse trailer, non-skid footing, and a halter with panic snaps for adopted mustangs. So far, the mare was tired and frightened, but she hadn't injured herself.

A heavy sigh reminded Sam that Aunt Sue stood beside her.

"I'm going to get some of that coffee," she said.

"I'll stay here," Sam replied.

"Me too," Callie said, and though she sounded wearied from watching, she still sounded hopeful.

When she moved closer to the trailer, Sam felt angry. Couldn't Callie see the horse was already frightened? Pressing close and staring at her like she was a zoo animal would only bring on more panic.

"What do you think you're—?" Sam began, but then she broke off.

Queen belonged to Callie. It would do no good to interfere. Even if the red dun lived at River Bend, it would be temporary.

At least Callie moved slowly. Wind caught the hem of her cloak, pulling it out behind her.

A snort made Sam glance back at the mare. In snatches, she watched Callie come. Her lathered neck curved, and she fastened her eyes on the strange figure. Then she looked away. Seconds later, the mare turned to watch Callie again. The horse didn't look suspicious; merely interested.

A *bond*, Callie had said. Sam didn't really believe that, but the girl was doing something right. Sam remembered when she'd first started working with Dark Sunshine and the abused mustang mare had stared at the barn, listening to Buddy.

Queen was giving Callie that same attention, and Jake—or had it been Dallas?—had said, "That's how you want her looking at you."

Callie's luck seemed to be holding, today.

Her fingers moved from her brass pendant to another necklace. The charm on this one looked like a tiny bamboo tube. As Sam watched, Callie slowly turned the tube end for end, causing a faint rushing sound, like water over rocks.

"What's that?" Sam asked.

"A rain stick," Callie whispered, then nodded at the mare.

Sam looked. The dun's ears tipped forward, flicked back, then stayed forward, testing the sound for familiarity.

The spell lasted until the door to the office opened

and the men and Aunt Sue came back into the blustery day. Bale-Tosser was carrying a long stick of some sort. Sam felt a jolt of alarm.

"This next part's gonna seem a little rough," Bale-Tosser warned Callie.

She took a deep breath, but didn't protest. "You're the experts," she said finally.

Bale-Tosser nodded. "Thanks. What we're gonna do is get a rope on her and reel her to the side while I use this." He paused, holding up the stick. Now Sam could see it had a hook at one end. "To get that halter out of the trailer. That'll keep me at a distance, which will make her happier. Besides, it's not going to do anyone any good for me to get my brains kicked out. Then, we'll keep her in position to get the halter back on."

Five minutes later, it was done.

Callie stood where the mare could watch her and listen to the fall of whatever was inside the bamboo tube.

Queen kept watching and listening, and this time, when the halter went over her head, she seemed more annoyed than scared.

"Whatever you're doin' worked like a charm," Bale-Tosser said to Callie.

"It's probably my talisman," Callie said, touching the brass circle she'd been fooling with before. "The engraving's of Rhiannon the horse goddess."

Sam had never heard of Rhiannon the horse

goddess and she couldn't believe the way Callie gave the credit to her necklace.

As far as Sam knew, a talisman was like a good luck charm. Believing in one was pure superstition, but Callie had spoken as if it was as common as a horse being attracted by a fresh red apple.

And now Bale-Tosser and another BLM employee were making a fuss over Callie because she could drive the truck pulling the horse trailer. She was experienced, it seemed, because she'd driven the big truck her parents had used for their health food store.

"I think I know where I'm going," Callie said to Aunt Sue. "But I'll follow you to River Bend, okay?"

"That's fine, but how are we going to get this horse out when we arrive?" Aunt Sue asked.

It was a good question. One look at Aunt Sue's tight lips and raised eyebrow told Sam to not even think of doing it alone.

"That's right," Bale-Tosser said. "Wyatt's on his honeymoon." He smiled and glanced briefly at Sam.

She shrugged and nodded toward Aunt Sue.

"I think the two of us can do it," Callie suggested.

"Not while I'm the reigning adult," Aunt Sue said.

Sam didn't argue. She didn't have a pinch of faith in Callie and her talisman. If they couldn't handle the mare, she could be further injured coming out of the trailer.

"How 'bout I call Jed Kenworthy and tell him to swing by in a half hour or so," Bale-Tosser suggested.

Aunt Sue glanced at her for approval and Sam hesitated. Jed was like Dad. A mustang had to prove its worth to them, and even then they doubted their own eyes.

"Or Jake Ely? He's a good hand with horses and I bet you girls know him from school."

"Jake's busy," Sam said quickly. "I bet Jed would help us out."

The last thing she wanted was Jake protecting her from a horse. If he and Aunt Sue swapped even two sentences on the subject of Sam's riding, she might as well donate her saddle to the state museum.

Aunt Sue wore her teacher face on the way back to River Bend Ranch.

"It was quite impressive the way Callie held that wild horse's attention, wasn't it?" she asked, then added, "she was getting a lot of attention herself."

Aunt Sue kept her eyes on the road, but Sam looked at her just the same. She knew what her aunt was suggesting.

"I'm not jealous, Aunt Sue."

"I didn't say you were, but Callie does seem to have a rather unconventional approach to horseman-ship."

"Horsemanship?" Sam squeaked. "It's more like snake charming. With a horse." Lousy comparison, Sam told herself.

"You mean the necklace?" Aunt Sue asked.

"Yeah, of course. It's like pure superstition."

"Nothing like that bracelet you told me about, I suppose."

Sam caught her breath. Aunt Sue might as well have said *gotcha*.

She'd written Aunt Sue a letter about the silvery circlet she'd braided with hair from the Phantom's mane.

"It's not the same," Sam said. "I think my bracelet works—if it does—because he smells it."

She was lucky Aunt Sue couldn't read minds. Sam remembered how she'd decided to leave the bracelet in the pocket of her jeans when she was at the church, dressing for the wedding. She'd left it, not just because it wouldn't go with the formal pine-green gown she wore as maid of honor, but because she'd known she wouldn't need it.

Of course it wasn't essential to bond the Phantom to her. It wasn't magic.

Still, Sam was glad she'd remembered to slip it out before she put her jeans in the laundry last night. But she wished she hadn't left it on her desk.

When she thought of how the Phantom had challenged her yesterday, she decided she'd better put it back on.

They were approaching War Drum Flats when Sam noticed bales of hay stacked along the roadside. They were all on the right side, as if someone was feeding cattle. That was unlikely, since most ranchers had enough sense to feed farther away from the highway.

Except one.

Sam wasn't surprised when Aunt Sue braked to avoid hitting the rear bumper of a champagne-colored truck driven by Linc Slocum.

Linc had purchased the vehicle just weeks ago, in order to go cougar hunting. The last time Sam had seen it, Linc had pulled up to the bus stop, jerked open the rear doors, and practically forced her and Jen to look at the dead mother cougar in the back.

Sam didn't want to know what he was doing now.

"Go around," Sam urged Aunt Sue.

"I recognize him," Aunt Sue said. She glanced in her rearview mirror as she started to veer around. Sam looked, too.

Callie and her rented truck were back quite a ways, but close enough that she'd see Aunt Sue maneuvering around something.

"He's the gentleman with the vivid Western language and even more colorful clothes," Aunt Sue said.

"Hurry," Sam said, but it was too late.

Waving his arms like an umpire, Linc stepped into the street right in front of them. The brakes screeched and Sam's head snapped back with such force, she wondered if her forehead would have hit the windshield if she hadn't been wearing a seat belt.

"Goodness! What a fool," Aunt Sue muttered,

then turned to Sam. "Sorry, dear."

"Don't apologize. Say any rotten thing you like," Sam encouraged her aunt. "He deserves it."

Sam could hear the truck Callie was driving draw near. It idled behind them as Linc Slocum wobbled up on high-heeled boots. Sam stared at his belt buckle. A huge chunk of turquoise was centered in a silver square half as big as a toaster. It nearly distracted her from his slicked-back hair and salesman's smile.

When Linc's face appeared at Aunt Sue's window, she did the polite thing and lowered it.

"Howdy, ma'am," Linc bellowed. "Hello there, little lady."

Sam's mouth had opened and she'd bet Aunt Sue's had, too, but Linc's delight with his own nonstop talk prevented them from responding.

"Bet you all are wonderin' what I'm up to, stackin' all this good alfalfa at the roadside, and you'd be right to wonder." He glanced at the truck behind Aunt Sue's minivan. Still, he didn't speed up his comments for anyone's convenience. "There doesn't seem to be any grass along in here."

Even Slocum couldn't have missed the fact that it was winter, Sam thought.

"Mr. Slocum, it's been down to thirty degrees, and lower at night."

"I know that," he said, as if waiting for further explanation.

"When it's that cold," Sam said carefully, "grass doesn't grow very well. You know how it's green in the spring and brown in the winter?"

Aunt Sue looked astounded and Linc looked as if Sam had gone off on a tangent.

"Be that as it may," Linc brushed aside her explanation, "I have some investors coming to check out plans for my new venture, Home on the Range."

The name was familiar, but it took Sam a few seconds to remember Gram's list. That's what she was supposed to call Mr. Slocum about. But what could that be? Sam bit the inside of her cheek to keep from asking.

"You know the sort of investors I'm talkin' about, ma'am," Linc said, winking at Aunt Sue. "They've got a lot of wrinkles on their horns and a roll of money big enough to choke a mule."

"Ah," Aunt Sue commented.

"I want them to see some local wildlife and I figured this would bring critters down into viewing range."

"But Mr. Slocum," Sam said, forcing herself to stay polite so Linc would take her advice, "the reason most people don't feed right at the highway is because it's dangerous. The animals cluster around the hay. They get busy eating and hardly notice the traffic." Sam saw her words weren't sinking in. "They could get hit by a car."

Maybe that had done it.

Slocum's mouth opened. His brow creased. With both hands, he hefted his belt and the belly it underlined. Then he wagged his finger at Sam and turned to Aunt Sue.

"Isn't she just the cutest thing," Linc Slocum said. "Softhearted as a newborn lamb and no head for business a-tall."

Chapter Ten

Jed Kenworthy's truck sat in the River Bend ranch yard when Aunt Sue and Sam arrived. The vapor clouding behind its tailpipes said its engine was running.

Jed stood near the round pen, obviously eager to get the chore finished, so he could be on his way.

As Aunt Sue parked, Sam heard Blaze barking inside the bunkhouse. Jed must have confined the dog so he wouldn't frighten the skittish new horse.

"Your Blaze doesn't sound happy," Aunt Sue said.

Sam nodded in agreement, pleased Aunt Sue was coming to like the animal she'd first dismissed as a dirty dog.

Aunt Sue and Sam stood watching as Callie backed the truck and trailer toward the corral.

Sam admired the way Callie drove, but she didn't admit it.

She resented the other girl's maturity, just as she

resented her adoption of the Phantom's lead mare. Her feelings might not be fair, but she couldn't ignore them.

"Her other plan fell through," Aunt Sue said, as if she knew what Sam was thinking. "There wasn't much else we could do."

"I know," Sam said, but she was more interested in Ace's plaintive neighs, telling her to come play.

"Later, boy," Sam called. Then, before Aunt Sue could read her mind anymore, she added, "I'm going to run over there so I have a better view when Jed starts to unload her."

She'd just reached the corral when Jed released Queen from the trailer.

He stepped aside as the mare leaped out like a huge jungle cat. She almost went down from the sudden impact on her damaged hoof, but instantly she was up. Swift and silent, she ran for the closest fence, then slid to a stop. Her head jerked up in surprise, scattering her dark red forelock over her face. The hair separated over brown eyes that blinked in confusion. Then she swung away from the fence with a snort. She ran up to another section of six-foot-high rails and stared at it.

At last, Queen returned to the center of the pen. Her barrel shook with a neigh of longing and Sam knew the mare finally understood. Although this corral might look different and smell different than the one at Willow Springs, she still couldn't escape.

Wind snapped Callie's velvet cloak as she approached.

"I understand that she's safe here. I wish she did," Callie said. With a soft smile, she added, "But she will. Isn't she wonderful?"

"Beautiful," Sam agreed, but she was watching Jen's father come toward them. He looked just as quarrelsome as Jen had at the wedding.

"Not a bad-looking horse," he said, as if he'd guessed at their conversation. "Too lightweight for my taste. I'd say she hard-wintered, but it's not yet January. Winter's got four months to go."

Sam knew Dad wouldn't like it if she contradicted Jed Kenworthy. He was a lifelong cowboy and foreman of Slocum's Gold Dust Ranch.

Still, as Sam watched the mare circle the pen in a long, extended trot, she thought he was wrong. The red dun stretched out like a Thoroughbred, looking lean and fit, not underfed. Could it be that Jed saw her through different eyes because he didn't like mustangs?

"No more meat on her than a well-fed needle," Jed added.

Sam laughed, rolling her eyes at the cowboy expression.

Jed ignored her. "Too bad about that hoof." He paused to greet Aunt Sue with a touch to the brim of his Stetson. "You all plan to have this horse here when Wyatt gets home?"

"Do you think that will be a problem?" Aunt Sue asked and a line appeared between her eyebrows.

"Well, ma'am, Wyatt's like most cattlemen. We like *usin'* horses, ones that earn their feed. Not meaning any disrespect," he said, grinning at Callie, "but most of these"—he jerked his thumb toward the corral—"are only good for crow bait."

For a minute it was quiet and Sam heard scratching from the direction of the bunkhouse. She'd guessed right. Blaze was locked up over there and he was eager to get out.

"Well," Aunt Sue said, clearing her throat. "I'm going into the kitchen to brew some cappuccino. I brought my own portable espresso maker," she confided to Jed. "Can I interest you in a cup?"

"No ma'am," Jed said, and Sam was glad he withheld his opinion on fancy coffee. "I'll go over and tell Dallas he can turn that dog loose. I don't think he'll bother this mare none."

Jen's father had only taken a few steps when he turned back.

"I was supposed to ask you if you'd take Silk Stockings out for a good run while Jen's gone. She said she'd appreciate it."

For an instant, Sam felt as she did while standing in line for a roller-coaster.

Sam nodded, but she didn't say anything. That meant she hadn't really committed to the offer, right? Jen's palomino was beautiful, but a little crazy. Jen's nickname for her was Silly.

Sam wanted to ride her, but she was afraid. "Aunt Sue is kind of weird about horses," Sam said.

Jed nodded. "Guess you'll want to help this young lady with her new horse, too," he said. "I'll tell Jen not to count on it."

"Uh, no," Sam protested. Jen didn't like Callie. She didn't want to give Jen, far away in Utah, anything else to worry about. "I'll see what I can work out," Sam said.

Then she turned to Callie. "It's not like I'm a great rider or a real horse trainer and you're just boarding Queen here," Sam said. "I don't know if—"

"Of course I'd like your help," Callie began.

"Queen?" Jed asked." Did you say that horse is named Queen? Kind of a high-toned name for such a sorry cayuse."

Sam and Callie both stopped talking. Sam drew a deep breath. Even if Callie didn't recognize the cowboy word for a pathetic-looking horse, she understood his tone. And it hurt.

As Jed Kenworthy chuckled, Callie seemed to shrink. All of the spirit she'd shown while doing her own adoption and driving the truck and trailer faded. She wet her lips, at a loss to answer Jed's criticism.

Sam wanted to speak up. *I think the name suits her,* she wanted to say, but she didn't.

The last thing she wanted was for Jed to tell his daughter that Sam was sticking up for Callie. Jen would think Sam had a new best friend.

After Jed walked off to see Dallas, Sam picked up on what Callie had started to say.

"I'd be glad to help with Queen. I'm no expert, but I know a little bit about working with mustangs."

"A little bit?" Callie said. "You're practically famous for it. Everybody knows you've worked with the HARP horses, and I saw the way the Phantom came to you, that day at the bus stop."

Sam felt herself blush at the flattery, but she was pleased. She couldn't think of anything she'd rather be "practically famous" for than working with mustangs.

There was a metallic sound as Jen's dad opened his truck door. Sam looked after him, hoping Callie wouldn't ask why the man was so mean.

Sam could only think of one thing, and that couldn't be it.

Jed Kenworthy couldn't be petty enough to ridicule Callie just because she looked different than most local girls. Could he?

"I'll go get poor Ace," Sam said as her gelding gave another longing whinny.

"He loves you, doesn't he?" Callie asked.

"Either that, or he wants to get a look at the new girl," Sam said, nodding toward Queen. "I'll be right back."

Ace was so excited to see her as she came into the barn, Sam made sure she reached over and snapped a lead rope on his halter before she opened the stall door. Even then, she stood slightly behind the door instead of right in the opening.

It was a good thing, because Ace seemed determined to leave the barn without her. "Hey! This isn't a starting gate," Sam told him.

The gelding took her warning to heart, apparently, because he circled back. The lead rope hung slack between them as Ace waited.

"There's my good boy," Sam said, but she wasn't fooled. "Oh yes, you're very sweet," she said as Ace whuffled his lips against her neck. "But I don't trust you as far as I can throw you."

Sam kept the end of the rope coiled in one hand, and the other hand closer to his chin as she took him over to Callie. Sure enough, Ace's strides lengthened, his ears pricked up, and he uttered a low, inquiring nicker when he saw what Callie was holding.

"Your aunt brought us cupcakes," Callie said. She smooched at Ace, but gently shouldered his muzzle aside. "You're cute," she told him, "but there's not enough for three."

Sam took the package Callie offered. Gram wouldn't believe the stuff Aunt Sue had brought along or that she was offering chocolate cupcakes before lunch.

"I don't have to go to work today," Callie said. "But I have to take the truck back pretty soon. What do you think we should do until then?"

"Well, this is where I try to think like a horse,"

Sam said. Ace slung his head over her shoulder and rubbed his cheek against hers. "Take a look at this faker, for instance. He likes me fine, but it doesn't take a mind reader to see his drooling has to do with the cupcakes, not me."

Callie laughed, but then her eyes wandered to Queen. As if the mare felt them watching her, she trotted to the far side of the round pen.

"We had horses when I was growing up, and my mom said I was good with them, but thinking like a horse? I'm not sure I can do that," Callie said.

"You already have," Sam told her. "When we were up at Willow Springs and Queen was all agitated from being loaded, you distracted her. You knew she'd be interested in the sound of your rain stick, and you were right."

When Callie began shaking her head, as if anyone with a brain could have figured that out, Sam gave her another example.

"And look what you just did."

"What?"

"You could have just crinkled up that cellophane wrapper, making a loud noise that would have startled Ace and frightened Queen. Instead, you folded it into a teeny square and slipped it into your pocket."

"It can't be that easy," Callie said.

"Not always," Sam admitted. "But if you go with your feelings and remember two things, you can come pretty close."

"What two things?" Callie asked.

"Horses are prey animals," Sam whispered, as if she didn't want Ace to hear. "In the backs of their minds, they're always thinking something's going to eat them. The second thing is, they only feel safe when they're in their herd."

"So she's probably feeling lonely," Callie said, watching the mare. "Or at least, kind of exposed."

"That's what I think," Sam said. "Consider what she's been through in the last few days." Sam let her eyes lose focus as she stared at the mare. For a minute, it was almost as if the horse's experiences were a movie. "She was probably left behind by the herd because she couldn't keep up. She must have been hurting and feeling abandoned. Then, if they herded her in by helicopter—"

"What would she think it was?" Callie wondered. "A noisy hawk, a giant mosquito?"

"Who knows," Sam said. "Imagine, when she smelled the other horses, but before she could get to them, she was trapped in a squeeze chute for shots and a freeze brand."

"I bet that hurt," Callie said.

"They say not nearly as painful as a red-hot branding iron," Sam said slowly. "I think I could stand the touch of something really cold easier than something really hot."

Callie nodded, but she was still imagining Queen's arrival at Willow Springs.

"And then, when they let her out—" Callie broke off, covering her mouth. "She found out that the other horses were strangers. They might not even have been nice to her."

Sam swallowed hard. She was glad Callie had begun thinking like a horse. She just hoped she wasn't projecting her own experiences on Queen.

"And then the food was all wrong," Sam hurried on.

"Oh yeah, they don't have hay in the wild, of course."

"And just when she was getting used to the weird food—"

"We brought her here," Callie said. "Do you think we should turn her out with the other horses?" Callie turned toward the ten-acre pasture. "I mean, you have other mustangs here, don't you?"

"Three of them," Sam said. "Including this noisy pony right here."

Sam traced her fingers over the light-colored patch on Ace's shaggy bay coat. The angular code wasn't easy to read, but it proved he'd been captured by BLM.

"And there's Popcorn, the albino out there," Sam said, pointing. "And Dark Sunshine, the buckskin right next to Popcorn."

"She's a pudgy little girl, isn't she?" Callie asked.

"She's in foal," Sam corrected.

Callie's cheeks turned bright red. "How stupid. Of course she is. When is her baby due?"

"In the spring, I don't know the exact date, but we're pretty sure the sire is the Phantom."

"How incredibly lucky," Callie said, as she looked back at Queen.

All at once, Sam wondered how she could have been so dense. The fine-boned red mare trotting laps in the round pen was the Phantom's lead mare. There was an excellent chance she was in foal to him, too.

In just a few months, Callie Thurston could own the Phantom's lead mare *and* his baby. There was nothing Sam could do about it. In fact, there was no reason she should, but jealousy sped through her veins like lightning and Sam decided she'd keep that secret to herself.

Chapter Eleven

Sam's mind spun with envy.

But Callie had just asked a question and she was waiting for an answer.

"I think we should leave Queen where she is," Sam managed. A breeze blew through just then and Sam was amazed at its frigidity. She pulled her jacket closer, but the wind seemed to slice right through. "We do have other mustangs, but if we turn her out with them, I don't think we'd ever get her back in this round pen where we can work with her."

"Ever?" Callie said. As she bunched her cloak closer around her neck, she smiled.

"You know what I mean." Sam tried not to sound impatient. "We couldn't do it without roping her and dragging her back."

"She doesn't need another trauma," Callie agreed.

"Besides, I can't rope, can you?"

"No." Callie climbed up on the fence and laid her

crossed arms on the top rail. She watched the mare watch her.

Sam joined her.

Callie sounded almost hypnotized as she said, "So we're back where we started. Given the kind of week Queen's had, what should we do next?"

"What would you want?"

Callie frowned, really thinking about it as they watched the mare lift her head and sniff. Sam wondered whether the sudden cold signaled snow. It could, she supposed, but the clouds overhead were dark gray, not white-bellied.

"I'd want a hot bath and a cup of mint tea. What's the horse equivalent of that? Just being left alone with a little food and fresh water?"

"Sounds about right to me," Sam said. For the horse's sake, she tried not to be jealous that Callie seemed to have a knack for reading Queen's mind.

Sam put Ace back in his stall, then helped Callie unload the hay and grain she'd brought. The wind was so cold, it felt almost wet as it snatched bits of hay and sent it blizzarding around the ranch yard before they could get it under cover.

When all the hay was stacked in the feed room, with the burlap bags of grain alongside, Sam sighed. At least Dad couldn't complain that she'd allowed a strange mustang to come in and eat their expensive food.

Soon, they'd scattered loose hay in the corral.

Sam suggested sprinkling a handful of grain on the top, so Queen would gradually get used to eating it.

Right now, the mare only wanted to drink. She kept her body turned so that her eyes showed over the top of the bucket. She observed them, closely, ready to run if they invaded her new home. As they let her get used to them, Sam and Callie worked out a schedule.

Callie had classes at the beauty college every morning, but she was usually finished by noon. Two days each week she worked from twelve until five doing haircuts, manicures, and other beauty treatments.

"For people who are brave enough to be my guinea pigs," Callie said. She rubbed her hands together like an evil genius, then pulled her cloak to cover both of them.

"They're not risking much," Sam said. "You did a great job with me, and I'd just had my head shoved in a horse trough."

"Really?"

"Well, sort of," Sam said. "That's a long story that I'll tell you later."

Callie's smile lit up her face. Sam could tell Callie liked her company and Sam realized she'd gotten used to the girl's pierced nose and dandelion-bright hair.

For the mare's peace of mind, they decided only Callie should try to gentle her.

"She needs to hear you and smell you and, as soon

as she'll allow it, let you close enough to touch her." Sam glanced toward the house and wondered if Aunt Sue had her binoculars trained on them. "I'll work on a way to convince Aunt Sue that it's safe."

"It's not, is it?" Callie asked, but she didn't look a bit scared.

"No, it's not safe, but it's not as dangerous as some people think. Of course, I had Jake's help—"

"Jake Ely, right? From the Three Ponies Ranch?"

Sam really hoped Callie didn't ask for Jake's help.

Sometime during the day, Sam had figured out how she was going to pay Jake back for dousing her before the wedding. She wasn't going to hurt him, of course, but Jake took himself so seriously, he needed to be taken down a peg. After her revenge, Jake wasn't going to be eager to hang around with her, for a long time.

Once more, Callie was waiting patiently for her answer.

"Yeah, Jake's been watching with every mustang I've touched."

Every mustang except one, Sam thought. The image of the Phantom shimmered in her mind.

"Well, I'd better get going," Callie said, starting toward the truck and trailer. "The truck's due back to the rental company by five o'clock. If it's later, I'll have to pay a penalty, and I'm not sure how I'd do that."

She sounded so grown up, Sam thought, but she

didn't know how to express her admiration.

"Thanks for saying she could stay here." Callie met Sam's eyes with heartfelt appreciation, and Sam had the feeling that if they'd known each other better, Callie would have given her a hug.

"It's no problem," Sam said.

"It could have been," Callie said. "I don't handle obstacles very well, but lately, things have been going my way."

Sam wondered how a teenager who was living on her own in a converted garage could think things were going her way.

"When my parents decided to move away and open a new store, I couldn't face it. I'd always wanted to adopt a mustang and I was afraid if I moved to town with them, it would never happen. They told me I could stay here, but only if I worked out a plan.

"So, I took a high school equivalency test instead of waiting for graduation and I passed. Then, I applied for a partial scholarship to beauty college and got that." Callie looked surprised by her own talent. "I don't know if I want to do it forever, but right now I think it's cool."

"That's amazing," Sam said. "I wouldn't even know where to start."

"Neither did I," Callie said, shrugging. "But it turns out that was the easy part. My folks give me some money, but I've got to pay for power, a phone, food, and all that stuff."

"Well, you must have done a good job budgeting. BLM doesn't give horses away," Sam said.

"My grandma gave me money when I got my GED and expected me to buy a car. I did, but it was a real bargain. You'll know why when you see it. That left me with enough money for Queen's adoption fee, the truck, and horse food. I'm going to see if I can work out some kind of a barter deal with Dr. Scott and Mr. Lake, the farrier."

"I'm not sure what you mean by bartering," Sam said. She remembered hearing the term in eighth grade world history, but couldn't remember its definition.

"It means trading stuff. I already scoped out Mr. Lake's wife," Callie said smugly. "And believe me, she could use a good haircut."

"Dr. Scott doesn't look like the kind of guy who cares about how he looks," Sam said. "He wears the same old jeans and flannel shirts all the time, and the only thing I've noticed about his hair is that it usually has straw in it."

"I'll think of something," Callie said. "Otherwise, I'm pretty sure I can live on noodles and oranges."

Sam knew Gram would end up feeding Callie. After one look at the girl's gaunt cheeks and thin wrists, Gram would be mixing up casseroles and baking extra batches of cookies for her to haul home to her lonely apartment.

The wind had stopped and the air seemed even colder.

"Good-bye, girl," Callie called to Queen. "I'll see you tomorrow."

She blew the horse a kiss. Sam knew they should stop talking. Callie should go home and she should go inside, but Callie was interesting , and Sam had to ask one more question. She fell into step with Callie as she returned to the truck.

"What made you want a wild horse so much?" Sam asked. "I mean, I love Ace and I'd do anything to keep him, but you made all these sacrifices before you even saw Queen. How come?"

Callie opened the door to the truck. It was a long step up to the driver's seat, and she waited until she'd vaulted up to answer.

"It's all your fault. When you stood in front of the bus to save—" Callie broke off and shook her head. "It inspired me. I don't know if I even want to ride Queen. I don't want her for a pet, either. I want her for a friend. Like you and the Phantom. Call me a copycat," Callie said, draping both arms over the steering wheel as she looked out at Sam. "But when I saw you with him, I knew I wanted to be part of something like that."

Sam couldn't believe she was to blame for Callie adopting Queen. Guilt washed over her again. Somehow, responsibility for the red dun's capture kept coming back to her.

But maybe, since Callie sort of looked up to her, she could find a way to make Callie return Queen to the wild.

"By the way," Callie said, as she started the truck and turned on its heater, "what were you doing up at Willow Springs, anyway?"

Sam decided to tell her the truth. "I came looking for your horse."

"For Queen? Were you coming up to adopt her?"

"No, I was coming up to see if I could set her free, but it turns out I couldn't."

"Why did you want to do that?" Callie's face turned pale and sickly. "Has this whole friendly afternoon been a trick?"

Had it? Sam swallowed hard.

It *had* started out that way, but now she liked and respected Callie.

She'd turned the question over in her mind for too long. Callie slammed the truck door and jammed the gear shift forward.

"Wait," Sam said, but the vehicle made a loud, huffing sound and the empty trailer banged as Callie accelerated toward the River Bend bridge.

Sam couldn't help noticing that even though Callie was angry, her driving wasn't reckless.

As the truck turned right, then vanished down the highway, Sam felt forlorn. The least she could do was check on Queen. But then she reconsidered. If she disturbed the horse again, it would be to make herself feel better.

She stood still a minute. She listened to the grinding of teeth. If Queen was eating, she wasn't terrified by her confinement or concerned over the wet smell of the evening air. Queen was fine.

Blaze appeared at Sam's side as she crossed the ranch yard. Instinct must have told him she was sad, because he kept shoving his cold nose into her palm.

When she got inside the house, she scooped dog chow into Blaze's dish. While the dog wagged his tail in appreciation, Sam heard running water.

Aunt Sue had started a load of laundry. She was also taking a shower. And when Sam returned to the kitchen, she saw a big pot of water boiling on the stove. She'd have to remember to explain the temperament of a country well to Aunt Sue.

In San Francisco, people rarely ran out of water. In the high desert, however, where it was hard, expensive work to drill for water, wells ran temporarily dry all the time.

Sam would have told her right away if Aunt Sue hadn't appeared with an outstanding plan for dinner.

"How does nachos and a green salad sound to you?" she asked.

"Fantastic!" Sam said.

"Nothing fancy. I brought chips and this orange goop," Aunt Sue said as she dropped a sealed bag into the pot of water boiling on the stove.

"Orange goop?" Sam asked.

"Instead of cheese."

City food, Sam thought. She wondered what was in the cheeselike substance, but not enough to ask.

She'd bet the original container had listed more chemicals than her science book.

"And I found some hamburger in the freezer," Aunt Sue continued, as she slid a skillet out of a cabinet. "I'll brown that and we'll have a feast."

They'd just seated themselves at the table and begun eating chips from the pyramid of nachos, when Aunt Sue stopped.

"Buddy." Her eyes rounded. "Your little calf . . ." Aunt Sue stared at the ground beef decorating the chip in her hand. "Will you have to give her up? Does she have to go live at, uh, McDonald's?"

Sam covered her lips with one hand, afraid she'd laugh the chips out of her mouth.

"That's one reality of ranch life your mother managed to make me understand," Aunt Sue added solemnly.

"Buddy was orphaned," Sam explained. "And Dad gave her to me to raise. So, no, Buddy won't grow up to be a hamburger. That's not true for all orphans, though. I'm lucky Dad made an exception for her."

"We always do for those we love," Aunt Sue said.

Something in her tone warned Sam that there was a lecture coming, but Aunt Sue waited until they'd almost finished with dinner to begin.

"I'm not sure I like the way your friend Jen behaved."

"By that you mean you don't like her."

"Not exactly," Aunt Sue said. "But at the wedding, I was concerned, and today—"

"Today Jen wasn't even there!"

"That's right, but I recognized some of the same things in you."

"You were inside the house," Sam snapped. "I don't know what you're talking about."

Then Sam stopped. She couldn't put a name to what Aunt Sue meant, but she did understand. Besides that, she'd better be careful. Aunt Sue was really nice, but she had a temper once she got going.

"I imagine it's much the same as knowing what a horse is thinking," Aunt Sue said. "I could read your body language. One isn't a teacher for half her life without noticing the way a girl tilts her head and puts her hand on her hip while she listens to gossip about another girl. And does nothing."

Aunt Sue had done a pretty good job of describing the way Sam had felt when first Jen, then her father, criticized Callie.

"Jen's parents are fighting a lot," Sam explained. "I guess her mom doesn't want to move back to the city, but her dad *thinks* she does. And her dad wants to stay on the ranch, but he hates being bossed around by a know-nothing like Slocum."

"Yes?" Aunt Sue encouraged.

"So, I think the whole family is a mess. I know Jen doesn't sleep well. I bet her parents don't, either. They're all worried and she's cranky," Sam said.

As Sam waited for Aunt Sue to see the connection, she poked a fork at her salad. They'd eaten most of the nachos and almost none of their salads. With a guilty twinge, Sam wondered what Callie was eating tonight.

"By not speaking out when they pass judgment on Callie, do you think you're making Jen and Jed feel better?" Aunt Sue seemed to be asking a real question, instead of just disapproving.

At the wedding, Jen's face had looked tight and tired, in spite of her nice velvet jumper. Today, Jed Kenworthy hadn't been his laid-back self; he'd been fidgeting and nervous.

"No, I don't think it makes them happier," Sam said. "And it makes Callie feel awful. She's just getting up her confidence to do stuff, and she's still sort of shaky."

"And what about you?" Aunt Sue asked. "How do you feel?"

Sam shrugged. She wasn't going to let Aunt Sue pressure her into admitting she still didn't really fit in here. She was afraid to offend those who did.

Sam was glad her aunt didn't push.

Aunt Sue stood, picked up the nacho plate, and her own salad bowl. Blaze danced around her feet as she disposed of the leftover food.

Then Aunt Sue met Sam's eyes. "Why don't you stand up to them, I wonder?"

Sam drew a deep breath. "I don't know."

Even Dad would say Sam didn't have the right to sass Jed Kenworthy, but when it came to Jen, he wouldn't back her up. If Jen's meanness kept up, pretty soon people wouldn't like her.

And the dislike might be contagious. Sam knew she'd already hurt Callie's feelings by standing silent.

"You didn't have any trouble setting Mr. Slocum straight," Aunt Sue said, chuckling.

She seemed willing to drop the conversation there, but she left Sam wondering why it was so much harder to stand up to someone you liked than someone you disliked.

All at once, clattering sounded overhead. Cougar's tiny paws pattered downstairs. Blaze gave one scolding "woof" as the kitten raced, wide-eyed, into the kitchen. Seeing them, he tried to stop, but he only succeeded in sliding across the tile floor with his striped tail straight up.

"Is he causing all that racket?" Aunt Sue asked.

The kitten made an attempt to crawl under the refrigerator, failed, then rocketed back the way he'd come.

All the while, the clattering continued, then pounded louder. Soon, it was hammering loudly, not only on the roof, but against the metal drainpipe that carried water from the rain gutters to the ground.

"What on earth is that?" Aunt Sue asked. "Hail?"

"I think it's sleet," Sam said.

"Oh, right." Aunt Sue turned to a cabinet and

took down a can of powdered cocoa and a bag of marshmallows. "What's the difference exactly?"

Sam thought of Queen standing alone in the round pen with no way to reach shelter.

"For the animals," Sam said as she stood and frowned toward the ranch yard, "sleet is a whole lot worse."

Chapter Twelve

"Samantha, please don't issue ominous warnings unless you're going to explain," Aunt Sue said.

Sam realized she was standing, holding her hair back from her temples with both hands. "I don't know exactly why sleet is so bad," she said. "I just remember everyone rushing around doing things when there was a cold snap like this."

"What kinds of things?" Aunt Sue didn't sound patient anymore.

"Running water to keep the pipes from freezing and going out to check on the range cattle. . . ."

Sam wracked her brain, but she couldn't come up with much else. "They must have just sent me off to watch television, to keep me out of the way, because I really can't remember."

Aunt Sue rubbed her index finger between Sam's eyebrows. Then she smiled. "No need to frown, honey. We can ask Dallas, can't we? Wyatt said he was the ranch boss."

"Yes. He'll know what to do," Sam said, then sighed with relief. "He might already be doing it. I'll run over there."

As foreman, Dallas made ranch decisions along with Dad and Gram. He'd tell her how she could help.

Aunt Sue stared from the kitchen window. Sam stood beside her. Here, the porch light created a golden circle of light. Over at the bunkhouse, another porch light shone. In between, it was cold and dark.

"Couldn't you just call him?" Aunt Sue asked.

"There's a telephone extension in the bunkhouse, but not a separate line. It's just across the yard." Sam pulled on a slicker and turned back to Aunt Sue.

"It's dark," Aunt Sue protested. "And the weather could be dangerous."

"I'll run," Sam promised, but when Blaze tried to follow, she ordered him back. "You stay here," she said, then opened the kitchen door.

She was met with a surge of cold. Icy rain hammered the porch. Chills ran down her neck and arms, but she knew she wouldn't get any warmer while she stood there watching. She drew a deep breath and plunged into it. Her boots hit a patch of ground that was slick as a frozen pond, and she almost fell.

"Running on ice isn't exactly what I had in mind," Aunt Sue called after her. "Be careful!"

"Good idea," Sam muttered. Compared to sleet,

hail was the pleasant texture of a snow cone. This stuff hurt.

Blackness and ice blurred the bunkhouse before her eyes. A golden rectangle appeared as the bunkhouse door opened and Dallas motioned her onto the covered porch.

The gray-haired foreman had the tanned and creased face of a career cowboy. In spite of his age, and the stiffness that flared up with each change in weather, he was unfailingly dependable and the best roper Sam had ever seen.

Usually he had the help of two other cowboys, Pepper and Ross, but they were in Idaho, visiting Pepper's family.

Now he wore a Stetson and slicker and was clearly about to go out into the storm.

"Why aren't you inside?" Dallas shouted over the pounding ice. "Get back over there." He started past her and Sam heard keys jingling. He must be driving out to check on the stock.

"Wait! I'm supposed to be doing something, aren't I?" she asked.

"You're supposed to be keeping your city-bred aunt out of my way." Dallas nodded toward the house where Aunt Sue stood with crossed arms, squinting through the sleet. "Wave."

"What?"

"Go on," Dallas said, giving Sam's shoulder a light push. "Wave to let her know everything's okay.

Then get back over there."

Sam waved, but she followed at Dallas's heels, wincing and wondering how she could have forgotten her hat. "What should I be doing, *really*?"

He started to get in the truck.

"Not much to do right now," he shouted over the pounding ice. "We're pretty much set up for bad weather. You could double-check the henhouse door and make sure it's closed tight, but the rest of the stock has the sense to stay under cover. I'm taking the truck out, to be sure none of 'em are in trouble."

"What about Queen?" Sam asked.

Dallas frowned in confusion.

"The new mustang," she added.

"That dun? She'll be just fine. She'd face worse than this on her own if she was out on the range."

"But if she was on the range, she'd have the whole herd to cuddle up with, and they'd be searching for shelter."

Sam remembered the time she'd hidden among the Phantom's herd. The horses had already been chased and nearly captured by a group of rustlers once. They'd been frightened enough to learn the sound and smell of the men and hide from them.

Mounted, but just as afraid, Sam had followed the wild horses into a brushy gully above War Drum Flats. The horses had been warm and dusty, all pressed together, and they'd taught her why they always sought the safety of the herd.

Queen didn't have that now.

"She's tougher than she looks," Dallas yelled, and then he was driving away.

He'd be gone a long time, Sam thought. Maybe all night. Together, the Elys, Jed Kenworthy, and Dallas would sweep across the range, making sure the cattle were safe. She couldn't question Dallas's priorities. Lost cattle meant lost money. Without the cattle, there'd be no River Bend Ranch.

She glanced right, at the ten-acre pasture, and saw the saddle horses crowded under their shelter. She looked to the left. Ace and Sweetheart had vanished inside the barn. Next, Sam hurried toward the round pen and peered through the fence rails. By the glow of the two porch lights, she could see Queen standing in the middle.

Why didn't Queen at least put her tail to the wind? Why did she stand there, facing the ice storm?

"What are you thinking, girl?" Sam whispered. "This isn't something you can stare down."

The dun's ears didn't even flick.

Sam needed a flashlight, a tarp, and a rope. With them, she could rig a shelter over one side of the corral and hope the mare took care of herself, as she always had before. The flashlight was number one on Sam's list. For that, she'd have to go back inside.

While she was in there, just to be absolutely sure she was doing what was right, she'd call the vet, Dr. Scott.

The radio played staticky music and the phone was ringing as she stepped inside the house. Sam shrugged out of her wet yellow slicker and hung it on a front porch hook. She would have wrung the water out of her hair, too, except that Aunt Sue was beckoning her to answer the phone. The kitchen's heat made her cheeks feel tight and hot, but she moved to pick up the telephone receiver.

Maybe it was Dad. It seemed like a long time since yesterday when he'd called to wish her a merry Christmas, and she could sure use his advice now.

"Hello?" Sam said, but then she felt her shoulders droop as she realized the caller was Callie.

"How is she?" Callie asked. "Should I come back?"

"No, Callie, I don't think you need to—"

"Come back?" Aunt Sue finished, as if she'd heard Callie's question. "Absolutely not. I've been listening to the radio and they say roads everywhere are too slick. 'Ice-skating rinks' they're calling them, and every few minutes they mention another car off the road. Some are upside down."

"Did you hear all that?" Sam asked Callie.

"Yeah," Callie's voice turned stiff again and Sam felt picked on.

Did anyone like her? Sam didn't think so.

Callie was mad. Dad was gone. Aunt Sue was disapproving. The Phantom had mock-charged her in a way that said he didn't want her help.

"So what're you going to do?" Callie asked.

"The minute I hang up, I'm going to call Dr. Scott and see if he thinks it's a good idea to string up a tarp for cover." Sam looked at Aunt Sue in time to see her lips press together in a cautioning line. "Of course I'll do that from the outside of the pen."

"Yeah," Callie agreed, as if Sam had a pea-sized brain. "Oh wait, is your aunt listening? Did you say that for her?"

"Right," Sam answered. "So, I'd better go."

They both said "bye" at the same time. Then, after an awkward moment of silence, they both hung up.

Next, she called Dr. Scott, but only got his answering machine.

"This is Glenn Scott. The vet. I'm over at Blind Faith Mustang Sanctuary and likely to be here until the roads clear. If you're calling about the litter of pups I posted at the feed store, I still have two of them. If you're calling about how to handle the weather, here are some general recommendations: make sure all stock has shelter. If this ice storm lasts, they'll want to stand still. Don't let 'em or they'll become Popsicles. This is especially important with poultry." *Beeep.*

The sound was so loud, Sam held the receiver away from her ear. Then the message resumed.

"Sorry about that," Dr. Scott chuckled. "Chickens' eyes have been known to ice over, rendering them blind. Lock 'em in their coops. Range cattle should find their own shelter, but you'll want to do heavy supplemental feeding for reasons you can probably figure out. Provide cover for penned animals, even if you just stake a tarp over one corner. If this is an emergency, call me on my cell. . . ." Sam hung up.

"I'm brilliant," Sam told Aunt Sue. "The vet said to do exactly what I was planning to do."

Sam was reaching for the flashlight on top of the refrigerator when the phone rang again.

"We're not ever going to sit down and watch *Casablanca*, are we?" Aunt Sue sighed.

This time it *had* to be Dad.

It wasn't.

"Hi there, little lady, this is Linc Slocum, with a favor to ask."

Before Sam could even respond, Linc launched into a one-man discussion of Mrs. Allen, her land, his land, and his scheme for Home on the Range.

Sam still didn't know what it was and she didn't care.

She only realized she'd slapped her forehead in frustration when Aunt Sue peeled her hand back to look into her eyes.

To calm her aunt's concern, Sam smiled and made a "no big deal" gesture.

"You still with me, little lady?" he asked.

"Sure, Mr. Slocum, but I couldn't convince Mrs. Allen to go along with your plan, even if I wanted to,"

Sam said. When she saw Aunt Sue's raised eyebrow, she added, "I'm not being rude, but I don't even know what you mean by your 'Home on the Range' plan."

"It's only the most elegant destination resort on this half of the United States. It'll be Western, all right, but no more like a dude ranch than a Thoroughbred is like a jackrabbit." Slocum drew a deep breath. "Why, our guests will fly in from all over the country—all over the world!—and land on my private airstrip. While they're here, they'll dine on meals created by a French chef, swim in my tropically landscaped swimming pool, and play golf on greens as smooth as velvet. And all the while, mind you, they'll be in the heart of mustang country and—" Slocum's voice broke off. "What *is* that infernal racket?"

Outside, the sleet came down with renewed force. It was typical, Sam thought, that Linc Slocum was oblivious to weather that could damage his ranch and harm his cattle.

"It's sleet, Mr. Slocum. I'm sure Jed is out checking on your stock and—"

"Shoot, yes," he said in a disgusted tone. "Came up here to my house and couldn't stop babbling about it. Don't know what he was fussin' about, with cattle a dime a dozen. And that old ranch house shoulda been bulldozed long ago."

"That old ranch house" was Jen's home. How could Slocum believe the cozy wood and river rock house should be knocked down?

"What's wrong with the Kenworthys' house?" she asked.

"Oh, it's sprung a leak, a couple leaks, or some such nonsense, but the important thing, now, is that you call Trudy Allen—"

Sam pictured Jen and Lila darting around, putting cooking pots under streams of water that managed to slip past the roof shingles. But they couldn't do that, because they were in Utah. And Jed couldn't do it, either. He was out in the freezing rain, trying to save the red-and-white Herefords because it was his job to care for them.

Listening to Linc Slocum talk about what was important was a waste of time. The man had no idea.

"Mr. Slocum, I'm sure we'll discuss this later." Sam tried to talk over him. "But right now I've got a mustang to check on. This ice storm is dangerous."

"—symbol of the wild West," he continued.

"Gotta go," Sam said, and hung up. She stared at Aunt Sue, waiting for a reprimand.

"You did a lovely job of handling that insufferable man."

"I've had a lot of practice," Sam admitted.

"Now," Aunt Sue said, nodding toward the hammering sleet. "Do you want some help with that tarp thing you're going to do out there?"

"I think I can handle it, but could you run water? Here inside the house?"

"Run water? Sam, you don't have to give me a little task so that I'll feel useful."

"It *is* useful. If we keep water running through the pipes, they won't freeze and burst." Sam stopped as she thought of Aunt Sue's shower and the load of laundry. "Of course, we could run the well dry," she mused, "but I guess we'd better face the problems we have right now."

"Sounds like a mature decision to me," Aunt Sue congratulated her.

"I'm glad I don't have to make them all the time," she said, thinking of Callie.

Sam pulled on her heavy jacket, her hat, then slipped the wet slicker on over both. She felt as clumsy as a walking snowman, and Blaze wasn't helping matters.

"You stay, boy," Sam ordered, but when the dog began whining, she took his brown-and-white face in her hands and scolded him more gently. "I know you want to help, but you'd scare Queen." She kissed the white spot on top of his head. "You can meet Queen later. Now, stay in the house and help Aunt Sue."

"I heard that," Aunt Sue said. Blaze wheeled to face her, wagging his tail. "And I do not need help from some uppity canine."

Blaze made a throaty, come-and-play sound and Aunt Sue rumpled his ears. Without stopping to wash her hands, she motioned for the Border collie to follow.

"Remember," she told him as he tagged along, "you can only watch."

Sam made her way through the storm to the round corral and found Queen standing in exactly the same spot where she'd left her before. Sam swept the flashlight's beam over the mare. The light picked up a sheen of ice on Queen's mane. Even worse, her eyelashes glinted with a glassy coating.

Sam wasn't sure she was up to another decision, but she didn't have much choice. Part of her wanted to slip through the gate, grab the rope trailing from Queen's halter, and lead her into the barn pen to cuddle with Ace. The other part of her was certain she couldn't handle Queen alone.

She knew what she had to do, and she could do it.

The wind had died down to a whisper in the tops of the cottonwood trees, and the sleet felt more like rain. Now, before the storm rebounded, she'd grab a tarp, some metal stakes, and get busy.

Then, if Queen still wouldn't seek shelter, she might call Jake. Maybe.

Not that it would matter if she did call him, Sam thought, hustling toward the barn. He'd be out on the range with his dad. With seven sons, Luke Ely didn't need to hire ranch hands to help run the Three Ponies Ranch. He worked his boys as hard as if they were getting paid.

As she snagged a large blue tarp from the tack room, Sam realized it was sort of cool, that even though she and Jake had had a disagreement, she knew she could still call on him for help.

Cool, but there was no way she was going to do it.

When Sam returned to the corral with her armload of stuff, Queen noticed. The sheet of blue plastic was already stiff with cold and it made a rattling sound as Sam threw it up over the top of the fence. She climbed up two fence rails, threaded clothesline through the brass grommets, then tied the tarp in place.

The sleet started down again, rapping on Sam's hat brim, but she worked quickly. Between the pounding sleet and the crackling plastic, she couldn't hear anything else. By the time she squatted to tie the last knot, she was muttering to herself and even that was hard to hear.

"Don't know why I didn't wear gloves. Stupid idiot fingers are going to freeze and crack right off if I don't get into the house really soon and . . ."

She heard something. It wasn't loud, just distracting.

At first she thought the sound was Queen's hooves. Then, she thought Dallas had returned without her noticing. It didn't matter which. As soon as she got this silly knot tied, she was going inside for a cup of tea. She wouldn't drink it, either. She planned to soak her fingers.

If she kept thinking of other things, this blasted tarp would flap her to death. She had to focus. At last, Sam blocked out the rest of the world and concentrated on the thin rope.

"Got it." She sighed, giving the last knot a tug.

That was when a voice one foot behind her boomed, "Nice work, Brat."

Chapter Thirteen

Sam let out a squawk at the same time that her knees straightened. It happened so fast, Jake didn't have time to get out of the way. Their hat brims bumped hard enough that ice chips rained down. They each reeled back a step and almost slipped on the mud underfoot.

"Why were you sneaking up on me?"

"See if I ever compliment you again!"

Both stood there, hands on hips, until Sam said, "What are you doing here?"

"You're shorthanded. I came to check on things. Dad asked Quinn to do it, but I beat him to the truck keys." Jake smirked, pleased he'd bested his next youngest brother.

"I'm doing just fine," Sam shot back.

"That's what I said."

"Okay," Sam rubbed her hands together.

Jake wore the same kind of yellow slicker she

did, but his was open over a flannel shirt. The shirt must have come fresh from the laundry, because she smelled some kind of pine-scented soap.

This was the Jake she knew, not the nervous dressed-for-a-wedding jerk who'd pumped water on her head. But he still hadn't apologized and she didn't think it was likely he ever would.

Sam turned toward the corral, clicked the flashlight to "on" and played the beam over Queen again.

"What if she doesn't go under it?" Sam wondered.

"She'll go," Jake said, but Sam noticed he kept his eyes fixed on the mare.

Sam glanced at the glowing numerals on her watch. For ten full minutes they stood watching.

Queen's muscles tensed, but she didn't look alert. Her ears drooped sideways and her eyes were nearly shut.

"She's light-bodied like an Arab," Jake said. "Built for warm climates."

"What should we do?"

"Give her time to quit bein' hardheaded, and—" Jake's shoulders jerked as if he'd heard a gunshot. "Aw, no."

"What?" Sam only heard a tiny tapping sound.

"Her teeth are chattering." Jake looked around the ranch yard as he closed the fasteners on his slicker.

Sam didn't know what Jake had in mind, but he was looking around for help. That made her nervous.

"Let's wait for Dallas to get back," she suggested.

Jake shook his head. "Can't. Look at her. She's forgotten all about us. She's concentratin' on what's happening inside herself. Stubborn animal could freeze."

"Let's call your dad on his emergency radio, then," Sam said.

Jake's father was chief of the volunteer fire department. He could always be reached by radio. Sam thought she had a great idea, but Jake's smile, white in the darkness, told her the suggestion was a mistake.

Jake's lazy tomcat smile was a challenge. "You don't think I can do it, do you?"

"Do what?" Sam kept her tone casual. Jake couldn't refuse a dare.

He yanked at the cuffs of his leather gloves, pulling them up to cover his wrists. He was probably looking at her, too, but his hat's shade made his dark eyes invisible.

"Go get me a bridle," he said. "I'll get my rope from the truck, catch Tank, and ride him to rope your wild horse. Then, I'll move her into a barn pen."

Tank was a bald-faced Quarter horse. He was usually ridden by Ross, and Dallas often wondered how the quietest cowboy on the spread had talked everyone into letting him ride the biggest horse. The giant gelding acted like an anchor on any animal Ross roped.

Sam headed for the barn, thinking. She didn't like the idea of Jake roping Queen. Sam grabbed Tank's bridle from a hook in the tack room and started back.

"Want her in with Ace or with Sweetheart?" Jake asked as he took the bridle and headed toward the ten-acre pasture.

"I don't want her moved," Sam muttered, but she couldn't tell him why.

What if the lead mare saw freedom as soon as she emerged from the corral? What if she escaped from Jake?

Jake stopped. He stood loose-limbed and waiting for her answer to his question.

Sam knew she had to go along with him. If she confided her fear to Jake, he'd think she had no faith in his skills.

"I can't let her freeze," Sam said, adjusting her sentence. She felt responsible to Callie, to the Phantom, and to Queen. "So put her in with Ace, I guess."

It was easy to hear Jake's boots moving over the frozen footing in the ten-acre pasture, and Tank protesting his separation from the other horses. When Jake returned, he rode Tank, but the gelding wasn't happy about it.

Sam aimed the flashlight at them.

Catching Tank probably hadn't been that easy.

Jake was hatless. His long hair had worked loose from its leather tie and hung behind his shoulders. He rode Tank bareback. One hand rested on his thigh, holding his coiled rope as he swayed with the gelding's choppy gait.

He could have been a movie hero, until he yelled at her.

"Cut it out," Jake said, squinting. "Point that light somewhere else."

"I don't think we should rope her," Sam said, suddenly. "How about just snagging the lead that's on her halter."

"*We* shouldn't rope her, huh? Care to slip in there and dodge her hooves and teeth? 'Cause I know I'm not gonna make a grab for that lead rope."

Jake's words conjured up a memory of Sam's fall. She almost felt the tremble of earth under pounding hooves. She fought a wave of dizziness and wondered when she'd quit being such a coward.

"Didn't figure you would," Jake said before she answered. "So I guess you'd better get that gate open and keep it that way 'til I get her back through."

Queen's breathing turned noisy as soon as Sam swung the gate wide enough for Tank to walk through.

Sam watched through the fence rails. Her fingernails sunk into the wet wood, ready to slam the gate if Queen bolted before Jake roped her.

The mare stood still, nostrils flaring and closing, uttering a soft, agitated nicker. She might have been talking to herself.

"Hey there, lady horse," Jake crooned to the dun

as she walked away from Tank. "Feels better to move around, don't it?"

Jake clucked to the mare. She glanced back over her shoulder, sizing up the intruders, and she kept moving around the pen.

"Wait," Jake's voice rose in surprise. "This is the Phantom's lead mare."

"Yeah," Sam said.

"You mighta mentioned that."

Only for a second did Sam wonder why he cared. Then she thought of how Queen had bossed and bullied the herd. Could she give Tank orders, too?

Queen's head flew up. Her muscles bunched as she sighted the open gate.

"Go on. Get on through," Jake urged her.

Sam got a good grip on the gate. She smelled sudden sweat on the dun, and felt her excitement. The mare was halfway through the gate when Jake's rope sang out and settled over her head. She hit the end of the rope, then hopped and squealed.

Sam used the gate as a shield. Her pulse beat in her neck. She thought of riding Blackie through that gate before he was ready. But this was different. The angry mare was no more than two feet away, but the wooden gate stood between them.

Sam knew Jake's plan was to follow the mare through, letting her lead him like a dog on a leash. With luck, they'd both be clear of the gate when Queen discovered she was still captive.

But their luck didn't hold. The dun figured things out fast. She planted her feet, furious that the loop tightened as she fought it.

With a quick change of strategy, Jake ordered Tank to squeeze past the dun.

Sam blinked back the ice blurring her vision. Was Jake planning to tow Queen toward the barn?

"C'mon, baby. C'mon," Jake coaxed, but the mare refused to be persuaded.

Eyes rolling white, the mare's neck moved with the tugging rope, but her knees locked. Her hooves stayed planted until the drag on her neck grew too strong to resist.

Instead of bolting after Tank, the mare reared onto her hind legs.

Sam gasped. She tried to believe the fence rails crossing her vision kept her safe.

The mare stayed in a rear. She used every ounce of strength to pull Tank toward her, but the big gelding didn't budge.

Jake did. First, she jerked him forward. Just as quickly, he hauled back on the rope, coaxing. The sound of his voice only made Queen fight harder. At the end of this long day, Queen had had enough.

Then Sam realized that with no saddle horn to dally around, Jake had dropped his reins. He held Tank with his knees, and used both hands to hang on to his rope while Queen fought.

Finally, she bowed her neck at the crest and

flexed, trying to break the grip of whatever held her. She didn't unseat Jake, but the extra exertion finally took a toll on her cracked hoof.

Queen groaned. Her off hoof faltered. For a heartbeat, a single hoof held her entire weight. Queen was about to fall backward.

Sam knew she wasn't safe. She'd be crushed between the gate and the ground by the thrashing mustang.

"Jake!" she screamed.

Queen didn't fall. Her forelegs came down, as if she'd quit resisting. The rope on her neck hung slack. Had Jake released her?

Queen tottered forward, gathered her feet beneath her, and swung away from the pen.

For a heartbeat, the mare stood statue-still. She'd never really seen the ranch yard. Bewildered by her surroundings, she moved toward the ten-acre pasture and the other horses. As soon as she spotted the fence, she veered left, toward the bridge.

Unsure and afraid, her hooves tapped in an anxious beat across the wooden planks, and then she was gone. Sam couldn't see or hear her, but she knew Queen was headed for the open range, with two ropes streaming behind her.

"What happened?" Sam yelled, but Jake didn't hear her. He galloped Tank toward the barn.

Sam ran after him.

"Jake." Sam puffed, trying to get enough breath

to make him hear. "How did she get away from you?"

Boots stomped and leather slapped. Tank snorted in surprise as the cinch yanked tight around him.

In seconds, Tank was saddled and Jake was swinging aboard.

"Tell me what happened!" Sam insisted.

She knew darn well he could hear her now, but Jake didn't speak. Tank was lined out in a run before he reached the bridge.

Go after them! Sam knew she should. Two riders make quick work of finding a lame horse trailing two ropes. But the mud around her boots was a slick slurry. Ace could fall. And maybe, just maybe, Queen would make it back to the herd.

They were a coward's excuses.

Sam gave up listening. She'd go after them, now.

"No way, no way, no *way!*" Aunt Sue was shrieking, storming across the dark, muddy yard toward Sam. She pointed her finger like a weapon. "You are not leaving!"

Aunt Sue made it easy for Sam to stay behind.

"Now, spill it," Aunt Sue demanded, toweling her wet blond hair when they got back inside.

Sam didn't want to explain. Too much had happened in just a few minutes.

"Sit," Aunt Sue ordered, pointing to the couch. "Not you," she whispered to Blaze, who'd obeyed instantly. "Her."

Sam sat, and ended up telling Aunt Sue every-thing.

When she finished, she was exhausted. She wanted to go to bed and pull the covers over her head, but she had to wait up. Jake would be back, with or without Queen.

The television babbled to itself as Sam and Aunt Sue sat side by side on the couch.

"So, you think Jake released the horse to keep her from falling on you?" Aunt Sue said. She sounded calm, but her hands were in fists. She'd bet Aunt Sue regretted her decision to let Callie keep Queen at River Bend.

"Yes," Sam said. "He's been way too careful of me since the accident."

Aunt Sue started to speak, stopped, then tried again. Finally she shook her head.

"I am trying, very hard, not to say something about what that knock on the head did to your judg-ment," Aunt Sue said. "Releasing a horse to keep it from crushing someone is not being *overly* protective."

Sam couldn't argue. Besides, she was doing her best to keep a few things about Jake to herself. She didn't tell Aunt Sue that *if* Jake had been riding with a saddle, this might not have happened. He'd acted like the worst kind of reckless, macho guy, instead of an experienced cowboy.

"I just hope he's okay." Sam's words gusted out on a sigh. "He broke his leg once when a horse went out from under him in the rain."

It was the wrong thing to say. Aunt Sue leaned her elbow on the couch arm and supported her temple with her index finger.

"Your father—" Aunt Sue shook her head. "Never mind," she said, and Sam sure didn't beg her to finish.

Blaze was first to hear hooves on the bridge. By his second bark, Sam had grabbed her slicker. By his third, she'd dashed from the house.

She needn't have hurried. The two horses moved through the dark in slow motion.

Queen was in pain. She could barely walk. She touched her off rear hoof to the ground briefly and lightly. Her head hung to the right, low in spite of the rope around her neck, trying to keep her balance. As she crossed the yard, her head drooped even lower and her limp grew worse, until she almost moved on three legs.

Sam's throat burned. She swallowed hard to keep from crying. It was an accident. No one was to blame. Not Callie for taking pity on a beautiful, lamed mare. Not Jake or herself for trying to keep the defiant mare from freezing. But she wanted to blame someone, even though she knew that Queen would probably be dead by now, if the BLM wrangler hadn't found her.

Ace neighed with excitement as Jake led the mare

to the barn. Sam could hear Ace turning from side to side along the rails of his pen.

Even when he dismounted, Sam didn't try to make Jake talk. Inside the barn, the lights came on and Sam saw his jaw was set hard. His eyes were as cold and unresponsive as Queen's.

The mare plodded into Ace's pen. She didn't shy when the gelding slid his barrel along hers. Instead, Queen stood still. The muscles bunched on her right side and she held her injured hoof just clear of the ground. When Ace sniffed her with great interest, she allowed it. She only flinched once or twice, when his attention grew too rough.

The lead mare made no protest when Ace stood beside her.

Queen slung her head over his withers and closed her eyes, glad to have a friend.

Chapter Fourteen

"Wyatt's first aid stuff in the tack room?" Jake asked.

"Yes," Sam said. "What do you need?"

"Something for pain until we can get Dr. Scott here."

Sam didn't want to tell him, but she did. "He can't come." She almost flinched at the hard look Jake flashed her. "I called earlier tonight and his answering machine said he was stuck at Deerpath Ranch."

With a quick shake of his head, Jake disappeared into the tack room.

Like it's my fault, Sam thought. But she didn't say it. She didn't even stick her tongue out at Jake's back, although she wanted to do it. Jake was like Dad. Both turned hard and silent when they felt powerless.

"I'll go inside and call, anyway," she told him. "He said he'd be checking his messages."

Sam heard the muffled rattle of pills inside a plastic bottle, then Jake finally answered her.

"Instead of that, how 'bout rubbing Tank down? Check his legs. He slid bad a couple times. If you find any swelling, deal with it."

Gee, what a genius suggestion, Sam thought. Yelling at Jake for being bossy wouldn't help now, so she didn't. But Sam really wished there was someone around to appreciate her maturity.

She took care of Tank. The Quarter horse seemed sound, only eager to get back to his friends. When she returned from turning him out with the other saddle horses, she found Jake squirting a pain-medicine paste into the corner of Queen's mouth.

The mare shook her head in weary resistance, but she was done fighting.

Sam could hardly believe it when Jake finished tidying up and started toward his truck. He hadn't said another word since ordering her to care for Tank.

Sam went after him, lengthening her strides to keep up. She wasn't sure what to say, but she knew she had to say something.

"Jake, it's not your fault."

"You got that right," he snapped, but he kept walking.

"It's nobody's fault," she insisted. "It was all an accident."

"An *accident* you didn't tell me she was the Phantom's lead mare, so she sure as heck wouldn't go where she was led?"

"I didn't think it mattered. You were only taking her a few yards!"

Jake brushed her words aside like a pesky bug.

"And I s'pose you just forgot to tell me she was already injured?"

"She has a sand crack," Sam began, but Jake countered her soothing tone by yanking open the truck door and climbing inside.

"Please don't insult me by sounding patient," he said. Then he closed the door in Sam's face.

"I could strangle you, Jake Ely!" she shouted. How dare he cut her off in mid-sentence?

Sam paced two steps away. She hadn't done one thing to make him act this way. She'd been handling things just fine until he showed up!

Sam turned on her heel and came back, yelling, "BLM wasn't too worried about that crack. Dr. Scott—"

Sam jumped back as she heard Jake put the truck into reverse.

"Some friend you are!" she hollered, then slapped the truck fender as he passed. "Ow, ow, ow!" Sam drew back her stinging hand and shook it.

As she stalked toward the porch light, cradling her hand against her chest, she saw the curtain on the kitchen window drop back into place.

❊ ❊ ❊

Again, Sam dreamed of falling. Circus music played as she tumbled through a star-strewn sky. Wind whistled past her ears.

In the dream, it was both summer and winter. She cartwheeled toward Earth. Below her, Dad was shirtless and perspiring as he mowed a lawn. She spun round and round, light as a snowflake, sure she was about to hit the ground and melt, but Dad was deaf to her screams.

Sam sat up in the darkness. Heart pounding, she listened.

Cougar was asleep on the quilt covering her feet. He made a tiny mew of complaint, but he didn't jump off the bed, just merely rearranged himself.

Sam stared at each corner of her room and saw nothing but the normal jumble of shelves and clothes and posters.

It was only a dream, she told herself, but the ugly sensation persisted. She reached around and touched the space between her shoulder blades. It wasn't sore. In her dream, someone she loved had pushed her.

She hadn't seen the person's face, but as she was falling and begging Dad for help, she'd been choked with a feeling of loss.

She scooted to the end of her bed and polished an opening in the frost covering her window. She looked through. She stared until multicolored dots frenzied in front of her eyes, but saw nothing out of the ordinary.

No ghostly horses galloped on the wild side of the river. No Phantom waited for her in the shallows of La Charla. A pair of headlights appeared on the highway. They moved slowly until a second set of lights materialized. Then, the first pair sped on and the second set slowed and turned in.

The sound of the pickup truck bumping over the River Bend bridge told her Dallas had finally come home. But it was the dream, not Dallas, that had wakened her.

The dream had seemed so real, but maybe her mind was just recycling the feel of falling from Ace. Maybe she was sick of making adult decisions, and needed Dad's help.

Sam sighed. She wasn't a psychiatrist or a psychic, so she'd probably never know.

Just then, a high-pitched neigh of longing rang from the barn. Sam closed her eyes, trying to block the sound of Queen calling to her herd.

Sam heard the scuff of Aunt Sue's slippers and smelled the scent of orange spice tea from the hall outside her room.

"She sounds lonely, doesn't she?" Aunt Sue's voice came from the darkness.

"Yes," Sam answered, surprised the sound had woken Aunt Sue, who slept to the hooting of foghorns and the metallic rumble of cable cars. Or maybe she hadn't been to bed yet.

"She'd be suffering even worse out in the, you

know, terrain," Aunt Sue said.

"Uh-huh," Sam said. In spite of her melancholy, she smiled.

Aunt Sue had a long way to go to be a ranch woman, but she was trying.

Sam woke out of a sound sleep to the knowledge someone was standing beside her bed.

"There's a man in the yard, walking toward the barn."

"Huh?" Sam sat up.

Her room was filled with sunlight and Aunt Sue looked down at her. Sam shoved her auburn hair back from her face and rubbed her fingers on her cheeks. Did improved circulation wake you up?

"I said . . ."

"What's he look like?" Sam swung her legs from beneath the covers.

"He's a young man with glasses and a very purposeful walk."

"Dr. Scott," Sam said. She replaced her nightgown with jeans, a thermal undershirt and sweater, thick socks, and boots. "He's a good guy," she explained. "He did such a great job at a rodeo, once, that Brynna put him on retainer for Willow Springs."

"The place we went to get the wild horse," Aunt Sue clarified.

"Yeah, but everyone around here uses him when they can," Sam said. Then she ran down the stairs, wishing Callie was here to listen to Dr. Scott's assessment of her mare.

"I suppose it's futile to ask you to eat breakfast first," Aunt Sue called after her.

"Well." Sam tried to be polite. "I shouldn't be too long."

"Would you be tempted by cinnamon rolls?" Aunt Sue asked as she padded after her in fuzzy pink slippers.

"Oh yum," Sam said. "With white icing you squeeze out of a plastic packet?"

"None other," Aunt Sue's voice teased, as if baiting a trap.

"Then I really won't be long," Sam said. She bolted from the house with Blaze close behind.

The Border collie was glad to escape from the house. Aunt Sue had heard a radio report detailing the number of household pets eaten by coyotes each year. She insisted she was keeping Blaze safe, even when Sam pointed out that Blaze was a pretty big dog to be eaten and had, in fact, scared off more than his share of coyotes.

Aunt Sue didn't want to hear it.

When they reached the barn door, Blaze paused. He whined, wanting to enter the barn for a look at Queen. But a familiar scent stopped him. Since Dr. Scott had given him his annual shots, Blaze had kept his distance from the young vet.

Blaze circled twice, scratched the cold ground,

then settled with a grunt.

Dallas and Dr. Scott had turned Ace into the outside corral and improvised a squeeze chute in his pen inside the warm barn, so they could examine and doctor Queen.

The dun's red coat was stiff with old sweat that needed to be brushed out. It was also wet with new sweat that said she was unhappy again.

Queen's head turned and her dark eyes glared at Sam.

She'd charge right at me, Sam thought, *if she could get loose*.

Sam welcomed Queen's anger. The mare looked a lot healthier than the exhausted, hurting horse she'd seen last night.

"Mornin'," Dallas said when Sam's attention stayed fixed on the mare.

"Good morning," she said, but when she saw Dallas's expression, she wondered if he had purposely left the "good" off his greeting.

Dallas's reproachful look told Sam a vet bill could have been avoided if she'd left the mustang in the pen, as he'd told her to do. Sam just knew that any minute Dallas would rattle off his "no hoof, no horse" platitude.

"Hey there," Dr. Scott said from where he squatted in the straw. "Sorry I'm so late, but the roads were lousy." He glanced up, peered at Sam through his black-rimmed glasses, then returned to his examination of Queen's hoof.

Dr. Scott hummed some horse-soothing tune under his breath. When he began talking softly, it took Sam a few seconds to figure out he was addressing her, not singing.

"Your message made me think we were going to lose her," he said.

"She was in bad shape last night," Sam insisted. "First Jake and I thought she was freezing and then she seemed to be in a lot of pain."

Dr. Scott nodded. "Sometimes they can turn around real fast. She's in good health and putting her in with other horses was a real smart move. Not that she's healed, by any means," Dr. Scott continued. "But a good night's sleep with her buddy Ace seems to have improved her physical state, if not her attitude."

He must have touched a tender place, because the mare's tail whistled in a horizontal swipe.

"Jeez, girl, you can draw blood with that thing," Dr. Scott protested.

Queen's lip curled in a threat, warning Dr. Scott the flick of her tail was nothing compared to the good hard bite he'd get if she could reach him.

Dr. Scott wasn't intimidated. He stood, wiped his palms on his jeans, and turned to Dallas. "Fish oil," he said.

"Don't tell me," Dallas muttered, then jerked a thumb toward Sam.

"Well, she's not mine, either. But since Callie isn't here, uh, what do you mean by saying fish oil?"

"I want you to try that before we do any serious repair work or hoof sealing," he said.

"That oughta smell just dandy," Dallas grumbled, shaking his head.

"If it works, it'll help maintain the moisture the hoof wall needs to be healthy," Dr. Scott explained.

"No hoof, no horse," Dallas said.

Silently, Sam congratulated herself on her prediction.

"Like I said, she's basically healthy, but lots of mustangs have vitamin-poor diets and they're dehydrated for days at a time. That's not good for the hooves. I swabbed some dirt out that was building up in that crack, too. In captivity," Dr. Scott said, "we can probably keep this from turning into permanent lameness. Out on the range she wouldn't have been so lucky."

Sam looked at the beautiful mare. Queen had lucked out. She'd already been left behind by her herd when the BLM wranglers found her. She might have found shelter from the weather, but prowling predators would have discovered her and flushed her from her hiding place.

Fierce and smart as she was, Queen wouldn't have been able to outrun them for long.

"So, do you think she'll be all right?" Sam asked.

"Probably. There are lots of things to try, these

days. Besides sealing, we can limit concussion—"

"Keep her off it, you mean?" Sam asked. She thought of the mare's headlong run into the darkness last night and cringed.

"Yeah, or at least limit overuse on hard footing. Some folks put in staple kinda things or fill the crack with stuff like Super Glue for hooves. . . ."

"The little girl who owns her won't be able to afford that," Dallas grumbled.

"But fish oil," Dr. Scott said, smiling and holding up his index finger, "is a real bargain, and I just happen to have some in my bag."

"Fish oil?"

They all turned as a pair of female voices questioned from the doorway.

Callie and Aunt Sue stood framed in the barn door. Callie wore a pale yellow smock over jeans. She must have just come from class. Aunt Sue carried a blue pottery platter loaded with cinnamon rolls. Wisps of steam rose toward the rafters.

"Wash my mouth out with soap," Dr. Scott said. "I shouldn't have said 'fish oil' in the vicinity of that heavenly aroma!"

Aunt Sue laughed. She looked the same way Gram did when she fed Dr. Scott. The young vet seemed eternally hungry. Aunt Sue separated two rolls and slipped them onto a paper plate for him. Dr. Scott moaned in delight.

Sam and Callie each took one. The rolls smelled

so good, Sam took a bite and licked her fingers before saying to Callie, "Wow, you got off early."

Callie popped the rest of her roll in her mouth, then twisted her watch around on her wrist and shook her head. "I made good time driving out here, but it's nearly one o'clock."

Aghast, Sam looked at Aunt Sue.

"I let you sleep in a little," Aunt Sue said, as if it weren't a luxury.

"So, you're the young lady who adopted this beast?" Dr. Scott asked.

From someone else, "beast" might have sounded critical, but he so clearly liked the mare, Callie smiled.

"Yep, she's mine," Callie said. "She just doesn't know it yet."

"When do you plan to move her closer to home?" Dr. Scott asked.

Callie bit her lip. "I don't know. I'm working on a deal with my landlord. He has a field behind his house. Nothing's grazing in it but old, dead cars." Callie shrugged, looking shy. "I thought if I offered to get them towed and, you know, kind of cleaned things up, he might not charge much to keep her there."

Dr. Scott nodded. "Sounds like a plan, but you should make it soon. Horses need a herd, even if it's a herd of one and that one is you." He pointed at Callie. "You'll never make her yours by boarding her twenty miles away."

Callie's lip had turned white from the pressure of her front teeth. Sam hated seeing Callie's confidence drain away.

"You can work with her here. Right now, if you want," Sam offered. Since she could tell Aunt Sue was trying to catch her eye to reprimand her, Sam stayed focused on the vet. "Do you think we should put her back in the round pen, Dr. Scott?"

"I've been thinking about that, and I'd like to see her try your new pen, here next to the barn."

"Aren't you supposed to limit distractions when you work with mustangs?" Sam said, thinking about the new open-fenced pen. "You know, keep them focused on you."

"As a rule, that's a good idea," Dr. Scott agreed. "But this injury makes her feel weak and desperate. In there," Dr. Scott said, pointing, "she'd be able to see out, and she might feel less trapped."

"Okay," Callie agreed. "I'm ready to start anytime."

Aunt Sue's lips parted. Sam knew she was going to refuse.

Dr. Scott must have noticed, too.

"Let's start with the fish oil," he suggested. He squinted into the depths of his vet's bag, then plunged his hand inside.

"That's the end of me," Dallas said. "*Adios*, you all."

In minutes, Callie sat sideways in the straw, rubbing a slick mixture on Queen's hoof until it was shiny and smelly.

Dr. Scott kept Aunt Sue in his peripheral vision. Sam could see him watching her, treating her like a head-shy horse. Little by little, he got her used to the idea of Callie touching Queen. Finally, he stretched and made another suggestion.

"Strangely enough, I don't have any other calls, just now," said Dr. Scott. "I'll be glad to stay and supervise while Callie gets the mare used to her."

"Are you sure that's a good idea?" Aunt Sue asked. Then she noticed Dr. Scott's glance settle on the cinnamon rolls again.

Since he didn't seem bothered by the odd aroma of cinnamon mixed with fish oil, Aunt Sue extended the plate so that he could have seconds.

"I think it's better than good. I think it's a spectacular idea," Dr. Scott said.

Then he helped himself not to a single roll, but, smiling, his fingers clamped to the blue pottery platter and he headed outside with the entire dozen.

Chapter Fifteen

Sam stood beside Dr. Scott, watching Callie stand just inside the new pen, talking to Queen.

Sam wondered whether the fish oil had made Queen's hoof feel better, or if she just felt more aware. Something had changed, because the mare danced in a high-stepping trot.

"What do you suppose?" Dr. Scott asked Sam. "That mare was ready to eat me, and she wanted a piece of you, too. But look, she's not the least bit angry now. Nervous, sure, but she doesn't want to hurt that girl."

Dr. Scott concentrated as if the two before him were part of an experiment. Every few minutes, he grunted and said, "Hmm, interesting."

Once Sam realized Callie was safe, she thought about Jake.

Payback time had arrived. She'd almost forgiven Jake for pumping water all over her on Dad and

Brynna's wedding day. And for being so protective. But he'd pushed her too far last night, implying she was to blame for Queen's escape.

That wasn't true and it wasn't fair. If anyone was to blame, it was him.

He'd been showing off by riding bareback through the sleet storm. If he'd had a saddle horn, he could have snubbed Queen alongside Tank and everything would have been just fine. He knew that, but he didn't want to face facts. So he'd blamed her.

Not only that; he'd refused to discuss it. Making Jake discuss anything was a chore. He was pure cowboy in that way.

But I'm pure cowgirl, and he ought to know that by now. Sam smiled to herself. Maybe Jake needed some reminding.

She didn't care if he called her a brat, a troublemaker, or even a little monster, as he had once when they were practically babies and she'd hidden his boots after they'd gone wading in La Charla.

I can take anything Jake Ely can dish out, Sam thought.

His high and mighty ways made her itch for revenge, and it would be best to act now, before school vacation ended and Dad and Brynna came home.

"The fewer witnesses, the better," Sam mumbled to herself.

"What?" Dr. Scott pried his eyes off Queen and Callie to gawk at Sam.

"Nothing," Sam said, then nodded toward the house. "I'll be back."

The first thing she'd do was phone Quinn. If she knew Quinn, he'd be real irritated with Jake. Their dad had said Quinn should come check on Sam and Aunt Sue, but Jake had beaten him to the truck keys. So Quinn, not Jake, had shivered in the cold looking for cattle all night.

Rivalry ran high among the seven Ely boys. As the two youngest, Jake and Quinn always fought to keep the other in last place. This time, Quinn would get some help. From her.

Sam was already gloating as she came into the house. This was going to be so much fun.

The Christmas tree and Aunt Sue's herbal tea scented the house as Sam came inside. Blaze circled around her legs, then jumped up, trying to lick her face.

"Down, boy," Sam said.

Aunt Sue was turning the Border collie into a pest. She insisted on keeping him inside, safe from coyotes and bad weather, but Blaze wasn't used to the confinement.

Sam gave Blaze a scratch behind his ears, trying to tell him she knew exactly how he felt. She'd risk a bit of danger for her freedom.

The thought stopped her.

She didn't want Aunt Sue shielding her from danger. The prospect of a headlong gallop, with the wind in her face and sagebrush slipping by in a gray-green blur, was magnetic. For a minute, she wasn't worried about taking another fall.

Sensing a change in Sam's attitude, Blaze bumped against Sam and licked her hand.

If Callie hadn't been working with Queen, Sam would have freed the dog. But Blaze had shown so much interest in Queen, Sam knew he'd disrupt the bonding session.

"A couple more days, boy," Sam said, then almost bit her tongue.

She was not eager for Aunt Sue to leave, and she would never try to hurt her feelings, but Aunt Sue's protectiveness had backfired. Both she and Blaze wanted things the way they'd always been on River Bend Ranch.

She was opening the cupboard for a dog cookie when she saw what Aunt Sue had left out for her. A pink bowl of onion dip sat on the kitchen counter, next to a basket of potato chips.

More junk food.

This was getting to be funny, Sam thought as she dunked a chip into the creamy dip.

"Thanks for the dip," Sam called into the living room where Aunt Sue was stretched out on the couch, reading a book.

"You're welcome. It's not a particularly nutritious lunch, but how often do I get to spoil you?"

Sam shook her head and crunched another salty

chip. In San Francisco, they'd had some junk food, but not for every meal. It was a good thing Aunt Sue was only spoiling her for a week.

Sam closed the door to the living room a bit before she dialed Three Ponies Ranch.

"Hullo?" the deep voice was Quinn's.

Sam decided it was a good sign. Two parents and seven brothers lived in that house, and the one person she wanted to talk with had answered the phone.

She revealed her plan without any build-up.

Quinn loved her idea.

"You know what makes it perfect?" he asked.

"Tell me," Sam urged.

"Jake's in town with mom. Something he got for Christmas didn't fit."

"Cool," Sam said.

"I could trailer Witch over to River Bend, but if you really wanted to make him crazy, you could ride over here, then pony her back. Make all kinds of detours on the way. He'd have to track you."

"Quinn, you're a genius," Sam said. She swallowed a giggle, hoping Aunt Sue wouldn't ask what was going on. "See you as soon as I can get saddled up and ride over."

Sam had started upstairs to get her riding gloves when Aunt Sue peered over the top of her book.

"What's up?" she asked.

As casually as she could, Sam told Aunt Sue she needed to pick up a horse at Three Ponies Ranch.

That was true. She explained the ride would take about an hour and a half, round trip. That was true, too. What she didn't mention was the fact that she was stealing Jake's mare, Witch.

Acting like a horse thief, even as a joke, wasn't the sort of thing Aunt Sue would understand.

Sam waited for Aunt Sue's protest, but it never came. Just when you thought you had adults figured out, they broke their pattern.

Sam took advantage of Aunt Sue's preoccupation. While she was still engrossed in her book, Sam escaped.

She wished she had an accomplice. If Jen had been home, Sam would have asked her to go along. Jen would appreciate this prank, since it was aimed at Jake.

Her two best friends didn't get along because both thought they were pretty darn smart. They were, of course, but they couldn't bear the idea that Sam believed they were *equally* smart.

Sam didn't disturb Callie. She slipped into the barn.

"You're moving all over the place, today, huh, boy?" Sam asked as she led Ace out of his pen and tied him to a ring for a good brushing.

Dad always said you'd save time in the long run if you spent time grooming your horse. Not only did you notice any little bump or bruise before it became a problem, but grooming restored horses' circulation, he said, and made them eager for the ride.

When Sam stroked Ace's back with the soft body brush, the little gelding loved it. He stretched like a cat, then extended his glossy neck and stuck out his tongue.

"You silly boy," Sam said, smoothing her hand down Ace's back.

He tossed his head, then looked back at her. His black forelock parted to show a white star and mischievous eyes.

Ace was ready to go. His mouth opened for the bit before she asked and he didn't stamp as she buckled the cinch. Tail and neck arched, he pranced at the end of the reins, pretending he didn't want her to mount, but Sam didn't believe him. He was only acting like a happy horse.

"Save a little energy for Witch," Sam warned Ace, but she wasn't worried. Ace and Witch had always worked together well. She knew today would be no different.

It was a perfect day for riding.

Last night's storm might never have happened. Winter sun had dried up all but the deepest puddles and the wind carried the fresh scent of sage.

Ace was in high spirits, so Sam had to pay attention, but she kept cutting her eyes to the right. She held her gelding at a jog, scanning the foothills that grew into the Calico Mountains. Somewhere up there, she might see a silver stallion.

Sam felt Ace tremble, just before he turned in the direction she'd been looking and slowed to a stop.

Her fault. Horses went where you aimed them, usually. Sam told herself to pay attention, but when Ace kept pulling at the bit and dancing in place, she knew something else was going on.

Then she spotted the Phantom. As usual, Ace had spotted him first.

The Phantom didn't move, didn't neigh, didn't stir a cloud of dust. He was as still as a toy horse. When she'd seen him like this before, he'd been watching over his herd. But the hillside below him was empty. This time he was alone.

Ace bolted toward the stallion.

Sam slammed back, then forward with the gelding's momentum. Oh no, that was all wrong. In taking her weight off his back, she was practically telling Ace to run. She sat hard in the middle of her saddle, tightened her legs, and yanked her reins. Another stupid move. Ace felt the pressure of her knees as a sign of encouragement and just pulled harder.

The ground ahead was dark. Here at the base of the foothills, it was wet from storm runoff. She had to slow Ace before she got that far. To do that, she had to stop making stupid beginners' mistakes.

Ace wasn't lined out in a full run, yet. He'd obey if she just gave instructions he understood.

Sam took a deep breath. She sat deep in the saddle, but didn't clamp her knees. She found herself drawing in, concentrating on her shoulders, ribs, hands. Ace faltered a step and she snugged her reins. He shook his head, even though the reins weren't that tight. He was listening.

Fear drained away as the gelding slowed. Sam sighed and realized she wasn't afraid. Her pulse was still pounding, and she felt cautious, but that was okay.

She'd handled this little problem. Deep in her mind, she had all the directions Gram and Dad had given her when she was learning to ride. And the rules worked.

All the same, Sam's hands were shaking by the time Ace stopped. He blew through his lips and looked back the way they'd come. He shook his coarse black mane and stamped.

"Don't act like *I* made us do this," she scolded him. "You saw him first."

Sam searched the hills again. Of course the stallion was gone. As usual, Sam's heart was torn in two by having seen him. His beauty and wildness excited her and made her glad he counted her as his friend. But she knew he was safer far away.

"Ready to keep going?" Sam asked Ace.

He lowered his head to munch some pale December grass.

"Excuse me?" Sam said, jiggling the reins as a

reminder. "It's not dinnertime, fella."

Ace gave a bored sigh and shuffled into a jog as if this entire detour had been all her idea.

When Sam reached the Three Ponies Ranch, Quinn and Witch stood waiting. Quinn's horse, Chocolate Chip, was fully saddled and ground-tied nearby. Sam would bet Quinn and Chip had just chased the mare down to bring her in from pasture.

Sam had rarely seen Witch unsaddled. In only a halter, Jake's Quarter horse mare was beautiful. Her coat shone the blue-black of a crow's wing. Her roached mane stood up in a crest, baring her powerful neck. Holding her coiled halter rope was Quinn.

"She looks great," Sam said.

"She's pretty, but she's lazy. When she sees a rider setting out to get her, she's afraid she'll have to work. She takes off, and to tell you the truth, she can run the legs off every horse on the ranch. Except Chip," Quinn boasted. "He's the only horse that can catch her, and he did it again today." Quinn made a smooching sound toward Chip. The gelding looked up, eagerly. "He's her full brother, you know."

The two horses had identical confirmation. Only their coats were different. Sam noticed that wasn't true for the two human brothers.

Quinn was almost the opposite of Jake. Jake's hair was long and bound with a leather tie. Quinn's hair stuck up in a short, porcupine-sharp crew cut.

Jake had his father's wide shoulders and muscular arms. Quinn was thin like his mother.

Once Gram had called Quinn a "string bean" and Sam had never forgotten the description, because it fit Quinn perfectly.

Only the boys' dark Shoshone eyes showed Quinn and Jake were brothers.

Witch greeted Ace with snorts and a stamp, but Quinn was in too much of a rush to be polite. He moved with bony energy inside his rust-colored fleece jacket, lurching forward, before Sam could dismount.

"Hurry," he said, pushing the halter rope into Sam's gloved hand. "Mom just called to say they were starting back."

Sam tried to calculate how long she had to ride home. The school bus took about forty minutes to travel from the bus stop nearest River Bend Ranch, down the highway to the high school in Darton. The mall was only a few miles past school and Mrs. Ely drove a speedy dark-green Honda.

Jake would be home in thirty minutes, at the most.

"I'll have to go the back way if I don't want him to see me riding along the road," Sam said.

"Good call," Quinn said.

Sam waved good-bye and started toward the ridge that ran behind the Three Ponies, River Bend, and Gold Dust ranches. Witch seemed willing to be ponied alongside Ace with no complaints.

"Wait!" Quinn called, suddenly. "What am I supposed to tell them?"

"I don't know," Sam shouted back. Since Witch was behaving, she didn't want to stop.

She felt a pinch of worry, though. She knew why she and Quinn hadn't already formulated some fib. They were both honest kids. Mostly.

"I know," Quinn called. "I'll get really busy mucking out stalls. No one will come near me then, in case I ask them to help."

"You're a pal," Sam yelled. She gave Quinn a thumbs-up with her rope hand.

That's when Witch remembered to be crabby.

She rolled her eyes like a rowdy bronc, then spoiled the effect by sidestepping. Her sturdy black forelegs crossed one over the other in a move so graceful, it looked like ballet.

"Just wait 'til Jake sees how gorgeous I'm going to make you," Sam cooed to the mare.

Witch's ears swiveled to catch Sam's voice and she blinked her curiosity.

Jake treated his horse with respect, but he didn't praise her prettiness or make a fuss over her. The Quarter horse kept moving forward, but Sam thought the mare wore an expression that was a lot like suspicion.

Sam felt a spurt of her old confidence as she rode toward home. She'd handled Ace's wildness when he saw the Phantom. She'd ponied Witch for three miles, with no problems. Even when a covey of quail broke cover and scurried across the trail in front of them, Sam had controlled the horses.

"I bet," she whispered to Ace, "that I can get up the nerve to go galloping before vacation is over." Sam leaned forward and pressed her cheek to Ace's warm neck. "After all, you got knocked around by those crazy wild ones and it didn't shake your nerve a bit."

A familiar neigh wafted up the hill just as the River Bend barn came into sight. Ace quickened his pace at Queen's greeting, but Witch turned balky.

"Come on, Witchy girl," Sam coaxed.

The black gave a harsh snort, reminding Sam that she was a working horse. She wasn't used to being coddled and didn't appreciate baby talk. Sam mimicked Jake to make Witch feel more at home.

"Hey, knock it off," she ordered, giving the lead rope a sharp tug. "We're almost there."

After that, the Quarter horse cooperated, but just barely.

Sam shifted her weight back a little as the horses descended the steep trail. Down below she saw smoke curling from the ranch house chimney, and noticed Dr. Scott leaving. His truck was just bumping over the bridge, toward the highway.

They'd come down too far for her to see into the new corral, but Callie must be finished sitting with

Queen. If she'd spent this long letting the mare grow used to her, she'd done a good job.

Sam wondered what Dr. Scott thought of Callie. She remembered Rachel's acid remarks at the wedding. Rachel had condemned Callie's parents as hippies. Jen had wondered how good parents could allow their daughter to drop out of school and Jed Kenworthy, Jen's dad, had been just plain rude to Callie. And though Callie seemed to trust Sam's opinion about horses, Sam hadn't been very nice to her so far.

Would Callie confide in her, if anything had gone wrong?

Sam and the horses were almost down to level ground when Witch stopped, threw her head high as her neck would reach, and sampled the air. Her nostrils vibrated and her sniffing was noisy.

Sam checked the brush around the foot of the trail, but there was no cougar, bear, not even a skunk to cause the black mare to act so wary.

Witch uttered a loud whinny. She was answered instantly.

Queen's neigh overlapped Witch's challenge. The tiger dun sounded so angry, Sam could guess at her thoughts.

Queen, lead mare of the wildest mustang band on the range, wasn't about to let some barn-bred female defy her.

A quick check showed Sam that Callie was outside the pen. Flashes red as flame zipped around the corral as Witch continued to taunt Queen.

Ace didn't need any directions to know his job. Even though he and Witch were buddies, he treated her like a half-grown calf who didn't want to be dragged to the branding fire. He dropped his head and plodded for the barn.

Witch outweighed Ace by so much and she pulled so hard, the little gelding was almost walking sideways. But he didn't give up.

Sam clucked to Ace in appreciation, then told him what he probably already knew. "Too many mares is never a good thing."

Chapter Sixteen

Sam hustled the horses into the barn.

Ground-tying Ace, she tied Witch to a ring for grooming. She watched the mare sidle around, slamming her rump against Ace's pen.

"Just letting Sweetheart know you're here?" Sam asked the black. "I don't think she could've missed you."

Gram's pinto had taken one look at Witch and headed for the outdoor portion of her stall. She was a proud old mare, but she wanted nothing to do with the clash between Witch and Queen.

Sam slipped Ace into his pen, with a promise. "I'll check your hooves in a little while, boy. Right now I'm wondering if I should cross-tie Witch while I do her beauty treatment."

Sam decided she would. Witch was unpredictable under normal conditions. With Queen out there calling her names, there was no telling what she'd do.

And the clock was ticking. Jake could arrive any minute.

"What's happening?" Callie asked.

She'd replaced her yellow hairdresser's smock with a wool jacket. It hung open, and Sam could see Callie's peasant blouse and brass pendant. The smell of hairspray that had swirled around her had blown away on the high desert wind and so, apparently, had her hurt feelings from yesterday.

"I'm getting ready to pull a trick on Jake, and I could use your help," Sam said. She ducked into the tack room, found a sturdy lead rope, then looked for a metal mane comb.

"I don't know." Callie held onto the doorway and shook her head a little. "Jake Ely? Is he the kind of guy you do that to? He always seems sort of solemn and shy."

Callie followed Sam as she came out of the tack room with supplies, then she added, "Can he take a joke?"

"No," Sam confirmed. "He thinks he's too mature for stuff like that, but I'm going to show him otherwise."

"Why?"

"Because he's too bossy. He thinks he always knows best, and he's wrong. He may look like a man, but he's a kid. And he makes some bad decisions, just like everybody else."

Callie looked uneasy, but that expression was

erased by amazement as the puzzle pieces of Sam's plan came together for her.

"Is this *his* horse?" Callie's voice broke. "You don't mean you stole Jake Ely's horse?" Callie drew a breath, clearly amazed by Sam's bravery.

"I didn't steal her." Sam searched her mind for a more accurate word. "I just picked her up for her hair appointment."

Callie's arms crossed. "I know all about hair appointments, and they're voluntary. This customer doesn't seem happy about being here. And she looks like a no-frills kind of horse to me."

Sam had to agree. Witch was a stocky working horse. She was beautiful, but nothing about her looked feminine.

"That's why this is going to be fun," Sam assured her. "Besides, it's not that big a deal. He won't get too mad or anything. Really."

Callie exhaled, slid her hand over Witch's gleaming shoulder, then shrugged. "Okay, I'm in. What do you want me to do?"

"Help me cross-tie Witch. Then look under that hay bale over there, and dig out that bag of pink ribbons."

Witch settled down and let Sam comb her mane, divide it into half-inch sections, and tie each section with a thin ribbon.

Sam kept waiting for Callie to help, but the other girl seemed preoccupied. Each time Witch bowed her neck a little, Sam could see Callie on the other side, pacing, biting her lip, and sawing her brass pendant back and forth on its chain.

She hadn't done that for a while, Sam thought.

At last Callie stopped, crossed her arms around herself, and stared toward the barn rafters.

"Dr. Scott doesn't think I should have adopted Queen."

"What makes you say that?" Sam asked.

"You heard what he said about getting Queen to live with me."

"But you have a plan for that," Sam said. "You're going to get the landlord to share that pasture with you. She'll be right in your backyard."

Callie's right hand covered her lips as if she were forcing herself to stay silent until Sam had finished.

"That's not all," Callie said, as if she hadn't heard Sam's support. "After you left, he asked me when was the last time I'd ridden and what kind of experience I had with untrained horses and he started using words I didn't understand. I'm not dumb—"

"Of course you're not!" Sam protested. Her sharp tone made Witch stamp and switch her tail, so Sam lowered her voice. "He didn't mean to make you feel that way. He's a vet, though, and sometimes he talks like a textbook."

"I don't know . . ." Callie's voice trailed off and Witch made the only sound in the barn as she tested the strength of the crossties. "Maybe he's right." Callie raised both hands to clasp around her pendant.

"I'm not that good a rider and I told you, I'm not what my parents call a go-getter. Maybe I've used up all my motivation, or whatever, and I'm fizzling out now."

"How can you say that?" Sam asked. "You have your own place, your own car, and your own horse. You worked for them. You're going to school, too."

"I know, but I didn't think this out." Callie swallowed so hard, Sam heard her. "I'd always wanted a mustang and when I went up to Willow Springs, I planned to adopt a weanling. Babies are supposed to be easiest to gentle."

Sam nodded, but she didn't interrupt.

"And then I saw Queen."

Sam got chills at Callie's words. She might as well have said, *and then there was a miracle*.

"I picked her with my heart, not my head. She's an adult horse used to having her own way. Maybe she doesn't need a family the way I do."

At last Callie looked over Witch's back at Sam, and she wore a helpless smile.

Sam met Callie's eyes. In the beginning, she'd wanted nothing more than to hear Callie surrender. But now, she couldn't let her give up. If Queen went back on the range, she'd die. And Callie was alone. She'd give Queen all the time and attention she could. Even more important was the fact that Callie already loved the mare enough to be patient and kind while Queen learned a new life.

But Sam didn't say any of that sappy stuff. Right

now, Callie needed facts to have faith in herself.

"How did it go in there?" Sam asked, nodding toward the new pen.

Callie thought a moment. "She seemed more curious than anything."

"Good," Sam said. "It's obvious she likes you. She wanted to chomp her teeth into me and Dr. Scott, but she just trotted around, showing off for you. At least while I was watching." Sam thought of all the time she'd been riding over to Three Ponies Ranch and back. "She didn't ignore you after a while, did she?"

"For a few minutes, but I think she was faking," Callie said, smiling. "Then she faced me and watched me and finally came up to within about six feet of me. But that took two hours!"

"Still, that's pretty good. This is all new for Queen. You can't give up on her."

"I'd never give up on *her*." Callie's voice turned high-pitched.

"Okay, put yourself in her place again," Sam urged her. "If you give her back to BLM, they'll have to find another adopter and it probably won't be in Nevada. Picture yourself traveling cross-country in a big horse truck. You'll be crowded in with a bunch of other wild horses. How are you feeling?"

Callie sighed. "It's frightening. She doesn't know where she's going and those other mustangs are just oozing despair."

"And if she doesn't get adopted at the new place,

because she's too wild and wants to give orders to all the other horses, they'll ship her off to one of those megapastures the government has in Ohio or"—Sam spun her hand in the air. She couldn't remember where those pastures were, but Callie's eyes were glazed with thought, so maybe it didn't matter—"or somewhere. There, the horses just stand around and graze. They're not wild anymore. They're like cattle. So, if you're Queen, how do you feel?"

"Lost." Callie was quiet for several minutes. In the silence, Sam heard Queen circling her pen. Her hoofbeats sounded impatient, but not painful. "Even though there's plenty of grass, I'd wonder where my wide, white playas went, and how the mountains vanished and why I couldn't go splash in the river."

Sam finished decorating Witch, while Callie stood thinking her own thoughts.

Then, Sam stared at Witch's mane. She'd been a lot more successful talking Callie out of quitting than she had been in beautifying this poor horse.

Suddenly, Callie laid her hand on Witch's rump, and crossed behind her, staying close enough that the mare couldn't launch much of a kick if she decided to lash out.

"Here, let me do this," Callie said, in a no-nonsense manner. "Jake could pull the ribbons off those little tufts you made in thirty seconds flat."

Callie did just that, then stood back with a fistful of ribbons.

"If you really want to make Jake nuts, let's try this," she said.

Callie's fingers flew, but Witch seemed to enjoy the attention. She quit shifting her weight from right to left.

"There," Callie said, hands on hips.

"You mean, abracadabra," Sam said. "That was magic."

Witch wore a row of tiny plaits. Starting at her crest, they looped along her neck like braided satin. Between each loop, tiny bows perched like pink butterflies.

"You want to see magic?" Callie asked, digging her car keys out of her pocket. "I'm going to get in my car and vanish. There is no way in the world I want to be here when Jake sees you've made his monster mare into a lady."

Sam walked Callie out to her car. As soon as she saw the battered silver Jeep, Sam remembered Callie had said she'd been able to get a car and pay adoption fees on Queen, by spending a check from her grandmother carefully.

"You see why it was such a bargain," Callie said. "Remember that flash flood a few months ago?"

Sam's stomach clenched in memory. She recalled it well. She, Ace, and a small herd of cattle had been stranded on a sandspit in the middle of the raging La Charla River. She and Ace had almost drowned.

"I remember," Sam said.

"Well, a guy in Darton drove this Jeep into a

ditch full of water. It went in nose first, and stuck. The guy got out, but the engine compartment filled with water and you see how the body got banged up." Callie touched a dented door with affection. "But it drives great and it's only two years old."

Sam was admiring Callie's determination when the other girl held up a finger.

"Hey, I meant to ask you when I first got here," Callie said. "What's Mr. Slocum doing out by the highway?"

Being a selfish, irresponsible creep, Sam thought, but she didn't say it.

"He's feeding mustangs so they'll come up to the road and look picturesque," Sam said. "He has this idea that he's going to make a resort or something. It's a good thing most of his schemes fizzle out."

"Oh," Callie stretched the word out and pushed her glasses up to the top of her nose. "That makes sense. You know Mrs. Martinez? She and her husband run the bank, I think."

"Sure," Sam said. Mr. Martinez had boarded his curly Bashkir colt Teddy Bear at the ranch while Jake schooled him.

"Mrs. Martinez said Mr. Slocum was looking for investors for a housing development surrounding a golf course. I wonder if that could be the same thing?"

Sam's pulse pounded faster. A housing development. And this time Slocum's silly scheme had gotten as far as the bank.

"Go ahead and meditate," Callie whispered. "I'll see you tomorrow."

Sam didn't protest that she wasn't meditating. Maybe she was. All she knew, as she watched Callie drive away, was that Linc Slocum liked the worst sort of progress.

He wanted to bring people here for Western beauty, then destroy it.

Sam sighed and thought about going inside for a snack. She wasn't ravenous, but she'd been pretty active. A cinnamon roll breakfast, followed by a chips and dip lunch wasn't the kind of diet that kept her going. Besides, she was curious to see what kind of dinner Aunt Sue had planned for tonight.

As she crossed the yard, a shower of rocks from the ridge trail made Sam glance back. And then there was a shout.

"Oh no you don't! Get back in that barn!"

Mad as he was, Jake guided Chocolate Chip down the twisting trail as if the gelding were striding on satin. But Jake *was* mad.

He hadn't taken time to change when he'd gotten back from the mall.

He wore jeans, a blue button-down shirt, and running shoes. Not boots. He hadn't even pulled on his Stetson.

Once, when she was a little girl, Sam had heard Dallas joshing with Dad. Dad had taken a spill off a new horse and Dallas had told him, "You look mad enough to eat the devil with his horns on."

Jake looked just that mad.

"Are you talking to me?" Sam asked innocently.

Jake shook the index finger of his right hand at her, but he was speechless.

Chip shifted beneath him. Jake's anger must be telegraphing through his knees into Quinn's horse, because the big brown gelding swung from side to side, trying to understand what Jake wanted.

Jake wanted to teach her a lesson, Sam knew, but the horse wouldn't understand that.

Sam stood with her hands on her hips, watching. It probably wasn't a good sign that Jake was riding Quinn's horse. Then again, Chip had been saddled and ready. And Witch had been missing.

Jake swung down from the moving horse in one fluid movement. He didn't look back for the ground, but he landed perfectly. Sam held her breath.

She could almost imagine heat radiating from Jake's face as he stared at her.

Then, remembering why he was here, Jake turned toward the barn.

Sam followed him, then stood in the doorway watching.

Jake didn't talk to Witch. She nickered, turning her head as far as the rope would allow, and blinked at him. Careful not to disturb his blameless horse, Jake smoothed his hand over her as he analyzed the intricate braiding and bows.

"What's this supposed to prove?" Jake's voice was quiet.

Suddenly, her joke didn't seem funny. If Jen had been here, or Quinn, or one of Jake's other brothers, it would have been a great joke. But just between the two of them, her prank stunk. And she didn't know how to answer Jake's question.

"It's payback," she managed, finally. "For the dousing before the wedding, and the way you blamed me for letting Queen get loose, and a million other things. I'm thirteen. You're sixteen. Big deal. You are not my boss."

Witch jerked back to the end of the rope. Her eyes rolled and her hooves hit the barn floor so many times it sounded as if she was trotting in place.

"Let's go sit on your porch."

"I don't want a big discussion," Sam said. "I just—"

"Oh no," Jake said. "You wouldn't have done this if you hadn't wanted a big discussion. Now you're gonna get it."

Chapter Seventeen

$\mathcal{D}$usk wasn't a good time to have a talk. As she and Jake walked across the ranch yard, Sam wished for noon or night.

She felt stronger any other time. In this half light, when the sun dipped behind the far-off mountains on its way to sink into the ocean, she thought of Mom.

The twilight memory that made her most melancholy was all around her, now. One night—she must have been five or six—Mom had allowed her to stay up late. She'd get to watch a Halloween television special, *if* she took a long afternoon nap. She had, and awakened at dusk. Sam recalled padding down the stairs in stockinged feet to the kitchen. Though she'd been stooping to open the oven door, Mom had heard her right away. She'd turned, hands muffled in oven mitts, to show Sam a lattice-topped cherry pie.

How could even sweet memories hurt so much?

Sam glanced toward the ten-acre pasture.

Popcorn and Dark Sunshine stood together under the cottonwood tree. At dusk, even in winter, the trees' leaves were edged with fading gold sunlight and it almost looked like fall.

Mom was gone, and so were Dad and Gram. For now. And the last time she'd been close to the Phantom, he'd charged. Shaking his forelock free of his fiery eyes, he'd looked as if he'd forgotten who she was, or didn't care.

She knew too well how something you loved could turn on you.

A discussion with Jake was doomed. She could either act tough, putting on an I-don't-care mask, or she could cry like a little kid. Either way, she and Jake wouldn't accomplish much.

She sat on the step, closest to the porch rail. Jake sat against the house, as far away as he could get from her and not have to shout.

Even in his city clothes, Jake sat like a cowboy. He hung his hands off knees that were bent and spraddled out. He cleared his throat, squinted toward the barn, then gritted his teeth so hard, a ridge of muscle popped up along his jaw.

"I don't know how t'talk to a kid your age."

Suddenly, Sam wanted to laugh. Jake didn't know how to talk, period. He understood horses and cattle. Flicking ears and rolling eyes told him all he needed to know. But when it came to people, he was hopeless. If this talk lasted ten minutes, it would set a world record for Jake Ely.

Sam decided to rescue him. "I fancied up Witch to remind you not to take yourself so seriously. I've got Dad to boss me around and worry over me."

Jake didn't seem to hear what she'd said.

"You won't stop bein' crazy with horses, will you?" he demanded.

He couldn't know about her nightmares, about her fear of galloping and falling, and she wasn't about to admit her cowardice.

"If you'd been paying attention," Sam told him patiently, "you'd know I have stopped. I haven't run Ace in—"

"Three days? Four? Since you took that spill?" Jake looked disgusted, as if she'd offered him a lie.

"I told you I had to do a sudden dismount. Not that I 'took a spill,'" she corrected.

Again, he followed his own thoughts and ignored what she'd said.

"There's a natural order of things," Jake said solemnly, "and when people interfere, there's a price to be paid."

Sam's mind echoed the phrase. *When people interfere with the natural order of things, there's a price to be paid.* Had Jake read that? Was it a bit of Native American philosophy he'd learned from his shaman grandfather?

"I don't interfere," she began.

"'Course you do. Take Buddy. That calf was an

orphan. You saved her. Later, you put yourself in the way of coyotes trying to eat her. That's the price. There's Blackie, of course, and those mustangs." He gestured in the direction of Popcorn and Dark Sunshine. "And this wild dun."

"You can't count Queen," Sam rushed to put in. "I'd be a lot happier if she was still out on the range."

"With that hoof? As cougar bait?" he asked. "I don't believe you. Not that you're the only one. BLM's just as guilty."

"Then they should assign the Phantom another lead mare," Sam said. "His herd's in chaos without one."

"That's just what I'm talkin' about! He'll pick his own lead mare, Sam. Just give him a chance."

Sam took a deep breath. Jake was right. Blackie was now the Phantom, a wild thing. He didn't play by human rules.

"Is that all?" Sam moved to stand up. "We're starting to talk in circles. That seems like a good time to stop."

"Thing is, uh, in the natural order of things, I'm afraid you might turn out like your mom."

Sam stiffened. Vertebrae from the base of her skull to the seat of her jeans lined up like a metal rod.

Jake noticed. He made a soothing motion with his hands, but he kept talking.

"When she died, she was doin' the same thing you do. You think about animals instead of yourself."

Hot blood must've rushed to her face, because it felt like someone had thrown a pan of scalding water at her. For a second, Sam couldn't speak.

Then, she couldn't stop.

"Are you trying to make me mad? Because if you are, it's working really well and I think you should get the heck out of here, Jake Ely, before I hurt you."

She shoved him against the side of the house.

"Sam—"

"I don't want to hear it! All in one punch, you tell me my mom was stupid, I'm stupid, and—"

"That's not it." Jake puffed his cheeks full of air and the gesture was so childish, Sam stopped. Jake opened his mouth three times before words came out. "Just forget it," he said finally.

"What *were* you saying then?" Sam dared him to finish.

"I'm saying that—they're animals. Just animals. You can love them, but you're more . . ." Jake fought to go on. "To your aunt, Wyatt, your gram . . ." Jake made a growling sound, then rubbed the back of his neck. "And, I'd rather not see you hurt again."

In the sudden silence, Sam noticed it was awfully quiet inside the house. It was almost full dark now. Shouldn't she hear the television or Aunt Sue heating something?

"Well," she told Jake, finally, "you don't have to worry about me getting hurt again. I'm done doing stupid things with horses. I'm afraid to ride now."

Jake laughed out loud, as if she'd released him from his solemn trance.

"That's great, Jake. Really, it's just fantastic." She shoved his shoulder. Then, because he kept laughing, she socked him. Hard.

"Ow." He held his hand over his bicep, but he was still laughing.

"I spill my guts. You laugh. What a rotten way to get people to confide in you."

"Lucky for me," Jake said. "Can't think of anything I'd hate more."

Frustration made Sam close her eyes and clench her fists. She tried to explain. "This changes everything, don't you see? I can't go riding with Jen. I won't be able to go on the spring cattle drive."

"You are the biggest fake," Jake said, sighing.

"Jake, you know something? If you weren't a large guy, you'd get beaten up all the time. Weekly," she speculated, "maybe daily. Your body would be covered with bruises." She took a deep breath, then put sincerity in every word. "I am not faking. I'm scared. I'm even having bad dreams."

Heavy footsteps approached the door from inside. They sounded as if Aunt Sue were warning them she was coming, and that almost certainly meant she'd been eavesdropping.

Jake scrambled to his feet as Aunt Sue opened the door. She didn't come out on the plank porch, just leaned against the doorframe, holding her mug of tea.

She'd exchanged her sweats for khaki pants and a tangerine-colored pullover. She wore bright lipstick and she'd brushed her silver-blond hair. Sam wondered if Aunt Sue wanted to go out for dinner.

Aunt Sue tapped her painted fingernails against her mug, then looked up with teary eyes. "One of the saddest things in life is to take something that gives you joy and let it get ruined. Your mother and I spent two years not speaking because I thought she was insane to live out here and she thought I was a fool for not understanding."

Aunt Sue shielded her eyes a minute before going on. "What a waste of two years we could have had together."

Sam and Jake met each other's eyes. Adults never made confessions like this. Neither of them knew what Aunt Sue expected them to do.

"Does that mean you don't think the ranch is so bad?" Sam asked. This might not be the right time to tease Aunt Sue, but the words just hopped from her tongue.

"It means," Aunt Sue said, with a sarcastic lilt, "I'm about to make a big pasta dinner and I'm wondering if young Mr. Ely would like to stay and eat."

Jake's face lit at the mention of food, but he hesitated.

"Then I could drive you home while your horses have—" Aunt Sue broke off, and her free hand spun in the air. "An equine slumber party."

For a minute, Sam thought he'd resist out of pure stubbornness, but Aunt Sue's next words did the trick. "Do you think one loaf of garlic bread will be enough?"

"I'll stay," Jake said. "Thanks for askin'."

Sam stood, planning to follow Aunt Sue, but Jake touched her arm and she stopped. "What?" she asked, suspiciously.

"You're not afraid of falling. You're afraid of being afraid."

"Whatever that means," Sam said.

"This is what it means." Jake lowered his voice until she could barely hear it. "I don't know another soul who's ridden a wild stallion — on the range. Not in a corral, not in a rodeo arena, but out in his own territory where he could run off with you, forever."

Jake's whisper gave her the shivers.

No one had seen her riding the Phantom. She'd been alone in Arroyo Azul and the dark tunnel that snaked through the Calico Mountains. Jake had to be guessing.

"I don't know what you're talking about," she said, brushing the porch dust from her jeans.

"Right," Jake said, then kept quiet.

Jake was a world-class competitor when it came to keeping silent, but this time Sam knew she'd win. She and the Phantom shared a secret she'd never tell.

"Don't forget," Jake said finally. "I'm the one who picked you up after that cougar attack. You were probably in shock, and you were for sure shaken up. Your jacket was ripped with stuffing flying out, but you came walking down that shale hillside, out of a dark passageway, looking like the happiest kid in the world."

Sam started to deny it.

"Don't waste your breath, Brat. You were flying. And we both know why."

That night, Sam dreamed, again, of falling.

This time the dream was different. She still cartwheeled through night air, still passed a silver blur of stars, but then she was plummeting into water. All around her, it flowed brilliant turquoise, and she was going down toes first.

At last, her toes touched the bottom. Her calf muscles bunched and she pushed off. Bubbles streamed all around her as she jetted up toward the light. And when she broke the surface, a hot orange sun warmed her face.

As before, Sam woke to darkness and the sound of Cougar resettling himself on the quilt beside her. She stroked the kitten's fur, but he twisted and turned, trying to find a more comfortable position.

This time, Sam's heart wasn't pounding, but Aunt Sue's words played back as clearly as if she were listening to a tape recorder.

One of the saddest things in life is to take something that gives you joy and let it get ruined.

Sam's sleep-bleary mind sorted through images as if they were snapshots. She saw herself riding across War Drum Flats with Jen, then catching Champ after Linc Slocum had fallen from the lively palomino. She saw herself riding through the snowstorm to rescue an orphaned foal, and then she imagined leading Teddy Bear home with an injured Jake clinging to the saddle horn.

She tossed to her other side, trying to make sense of it all.

"Too tired," Sam murmured to Cougar.

Claws sheathed inside a velvety paw, the kitten gave Sam's cheek a gentle bat.

"Does that mean 'shut up'?" Sam asked.

She pulled the sleepy kitten into a hug.

"Mrow," Cougar said, and together they slept.

Chapter Eighteen

$\mathcal{E}$arly the next morning, Quinn called to tell Sam that her joke had gotten him in trouble.

"Jake's threatening to tell Dad how I helped you, unless I come over for Chip and Witch. Brian's driving into Darton to the library around noon, so he's gonna drop me and I'll need to ride Chip and pony Witch home."

"Sorry," Sam said. "I didn't mean for you to suffer."

"I haven't suffered much yet." Quinn laughed. "And it woulda been worth it if I coulda been there when Jake found his horse. You've got to tell me all about it. When I asked him, all he said was she looked like someone's pet poodle."

"She looked cute," Sam protested, but Quinn was already saying good-bye.

Sam hung up, took a bite of the quiche Aunt Sue had made for breakfast and decided the least she could do was catch Chocolate Chip and Witch before

Quinn arrived. Jake had put them into the ten-acre pasture with the other saddle horses before he left last night.

The phone rang as she was washing her plate.

"Hi honey, I miss you." Dad's voice sounded younger than Sam had ever heard it.

"I miss you, too, Daddy," Sam said, realizing she'd used her childhood name for him. "But we're fine. Are you having fun?"

"Big fun," he said. "Walking all over this town. So much that I had to get new shoes."

Sam smiled as she imagined Dad strolling hilly San Francisco in his cowboy boots.

"Are you shopping and going to plays?" she asked.

"Yeah, and hitting the aquarium and museums, too. Brynna's leading me around like a sow on a string," he said, but laughter filled his voice. "Things okay there?"

"Just fine," she said. Her eyes met Aunt Sue's. Would her aunt tell Dad about Queen?

"Weather okay?"

"We had some sleet, but Dallas and the Elys went out and checked on the stock. Today's gray and overcast, but it looks like the sun will burn through in a little while. Everything's fine."

"Good," Dad said.

Sam told herself it was just guilt that made her think she heard a tinge of suspicion in Dad's voice.

She heard Brynna speaking in the background

before Dad added, "So, if we decided to rent a car and drive back home, that wouldn't be a problem?"

"I don't think so," Sam said. "We're doing fine."

Sam realized she'd said *fine* way too many times. She had to quit. If Dad hadn't started out suspicious, she'd make him that way.

"Uh, Brynna wants to talk with you," Dad said, and there was a jumble of sound as the receiver was passed along.

"Sam!" Brynna sounded like a cheerleader. Enthusiasm bubbled in her voice. "How are the horses? Did you go up to Willow Springs? Is Norman White—?" Brynna's voice broke off. "Okay, your dad just reminded me we've only been gone a couple days and it's unlikely Norman White could reduce the entire BLM to rubble so fast."

"He was okay," Sam said. "But hey, it's *not* okay, is it, for Linc Slocum to be feeding mustangs out next to the highway? He wants some guests of his to see them. He—"

"Definitely not okay," Brynna's voice turned clipped and official. "If the horses stumble upon supplemental feeding for cattle, or if there's an emergency hay drop, that's one thing, but if you see him doing it, call Norman White right away."

Next Dad wanted to talk with Aunt Sue.

Sam had almost made it out the kitchen door to the stable when Aunt Sue hung up the phone and called her back.

"One hour of housework, then the day is yours," Aunt Sue told her. "Dallas is feeding the animals before he goes to Clara's for coffee, so don't even think of using that excuse. When we're finished, I plan to drive into Alkali or Darton, or wherever I have to go to get what I need to make peanut brittle."

"That's Dad's favorite!" Sam said.

"Louise mentioned that once," Aunt Sue said. "And there's no reason I shouldn't whip some up for him. I could wait and send him some from the city, but I'm learning it's not always a good idea to wait."

Aunt Sue held her arms open and Sam met her hug halfway. For a full minute, Aunt Sue rested her cheek atop Sam's head. Then she held her back at arm's length.

"Now, my little Cinderella," Aunt Sue said, using her fingers to comb the hair back from Sam's eyes. "Get in there and make that kitchen shine."

The house looked pretty good at the end of the hour, and Sam promised she'd help keep it that way until Dad and Brynna returned. Next, she called Willow Springs to tell Mr. White what Slocum was up to. When no one answered, she left a message on Mr. White's answering machine and hoped he'd check it soon.

As soon as Aunt Sue drove off in her minivan, Sam released Blaze from the house.

"Go get 'em!" Sam cheered the dog on. There

wasn't anyone or anything that needed "getting," but the Border collie searched nonetheless.

Blaze ran three circuits of the ranch yard, passing the chicken coop, swerving left in front of the barn, veering toward the bunkhouse, then back to the front porch to start over again.

As much as he liked the scraps and tidbits Aunt Sue tossed him, Blaze would probably be glad to return to his routine once she left.

Because she'd entangled Quinn in getting back at Jake, Sam was determined to have Chocolate Chip caught, brushed, and saddled when Quinn arrived. It was the least she could do, and it turned out to be a fairly simple chore. When Strawberry trotted up to see what Sam was doing in the pasture, Chip followed.

Catching Witch, however, was impossible.

When Callie arrived to work with Queen, Sam was approaching the black mare, shaking a measure of grain in a coffee can.

Afraid to wave "hi" with the hand holding the lead rope, Sam just lifted her chin toward Callie when the girl yelled a greeting out her Jeep window.

Eyes fixed on Witch, Sam heard the Jeep stop and its door slam. Then the pen gate opened. She didn't hear it latch into place behind Callie.

That wasn't good. She listened for Callie to check the latch. She might have missed it, because Witch was showing a little interest. She was still halfway across the pasture, but Witch extended her neck and her head jerked upward with a hungry snort.

Even if the gate hadn't latched, it might be for the best. Queen had never charged Callie, but there was always a first time, and no one was at the gate standing guard. If she was in danger, Callie might race for the gate instead of climbing up and over the fence.

For safety's sake, Sam knew she should be over there, watching Callie and Queen. She'd give Witch five more minutes to cooperate.

"Come on, Witch. I've got some sweet grain here. Smell that molasses? Oh yum."

Witch's ears flicked forward, then back. She swished her tail, flashed her teeth at Dark Sunshine, then crossed the pasture to stand beside old Amigo.

Dallas's sorrel gelding had gray around his eyes and muzzle. As Witch stood near him, the veteran cow pony's lips moved. When Witch tossed her head and snorted, Sam imagined Witch was telling Amigo how insulted she was that Sam would think she'd fall for *that* ancient trick.

Sam decided she'd just have to let Quinn catch Witch.

"You win," Sam called out to the black mare. "But Quinn will be here soon, and he won't put up with your nonsense."

Sam was halfway between the big pasture and the barn when she noticed Blaze. Head and tail low, he skulked toward the new pen where Callie was working with Queen.

"Blaze!" Sam called out, but the dog paced faster. "Get over here!"

She slapped her hand against the side seam of her jeans, trying to break the dog's concentration, but he ignored her and broke into a trot.

Sam increased her pace. She saw a flash of red through the fence rails and heard Queen moving restlessly.

Sam didn't want to yell and scare the dun. Queen could bolt into Callie and injure her. But she had to warn Callie to close the gate.

Don't be silly, she told herself. He's not going to start yapping and scare Queen. He won't flatten himself and slip under the lowest fence rail to sneak in, either.

He's a ranch dog. He knows how to act around horses. But Blaze had been Aunt Sue's prisoner for days. He might not be himself right now.

By the time Sam figured out what Blaze was up to, it was too late to stop him.

The Border collie trotted to the unlatched gate and jumped up.

Sam broke into a full run. Please let me get there first, she thought.

Blaze jumped a second time, and Sam knew for sure that he intended to slip into the pen and investigate the new horse.

"No!" Callie shouted from inside the pen as the gate opened.

Blaze jumped back with a yelp. The gate slammed wide, just as it had before when she'd been opening it for Jake.

This time Queen knew exactly what to do. She stampeded through the opening, alone. A lead rope streamed behind her. Sam ran to grab it, but she couldn't get near the mare. Queen didn't detour near the ten-acre pasture. Before, she'd hesitated, but now she knew the way out and she was headed for home.

"I tried to hold on!" Callie staggered out of the pen. Her forearms were skinned and bleeding.

"Are you okay?" Sam shouted.

"*I'm* okay, but her hoof—"

Chocolate Chip was saddled and tied near the front porch.

"I'll go after her," Sam said.

The big brown gelding tossed his head with excitement. He neighed and pulled, agitated by all the commotion.

"We can't let her run on that hoof!" Callie cried.

"I know! Call Jake," Sam yelled, trying to approach the eager horse. "Call Mr. White, or anybody."

"I want to come with you," Callie insisted.

"Go saddle Ace," Sam said, as she petted Chip's neck. She didn't shout, so maybe Callie didn't hear, but she had her hands full right now.

Quinn had boasted his gelding was fast, the only horse that could catch Witch. That meant Chip would have no trouble catching up with Queen. If only Quinn was here to ride.

"Settle down," Sam ordered, and Chip did. His hooves stuttered in place, but he was eager for her to mount. He snorted and looked back at her.

Sam put her hands on her hips and met the gelding's eyes. She'd been home for seven months. She knew how to ride. Even in new situations, the old rules applied. And rule number one was that there was only one leader in the herd.

"I'm taking charge, Chip," Sam told the gelding. "I can do this."

She jammed the toe of her left boot into the saddle stirrup. The leather was adjusted for Quinn and it was way too long.

For an instant, Sam considered riding with the stirrups that way. She could still climb up into the saddle, but she remembered how Jake had ridden bareback. What a disaster. Riding with flapping stirrups would be equally foolhardy.

Working quickly, she took both stirrups up. She slipped the bit into Chip's mouth and unsnapped the rope holding him to the hitching rail. Then she swung into the saddle.

The horse swerved in a wide arc. Sam had a hard time keeping her seat as Chip turned toward the bridge like a barrel racer headed for the way out.

The big brown horse moved into a hammering trot before Sam gave him a signal to go. She had to let him know she was the boss. Sam gathered her reins and sat into him.

"We're going to run, Chip," she told him. "But we'll do it when I say so, got it?"

The horse lifted his head and knees. He snorted and pranced, then settled into a perfectly collected lope.

Nice, Sam thought. *Maybe I'll live through this after all.*

Coming off the bridge, Sam wished she'd asked Jake where he'd found Queen the first time. Horses were creatures of habit.

But it was too late for regret. Sam leaned right, deciding the mare would have run along the river on this side, rather than try to cross over on her damaged hoof.

She saw horses.

At first Sam thought Queen had crossed the highway to the hay bales left by Slocum. Even from this distance, she knew none of the horses was Queen. Maybe the lead mare had headed toward Gold Dust Ranch where there were lots of other horses to command.

Feeling her indecision, Chip pulled toward the river.

"I'm still here," she told him, and used her hands and legs to underline the message.

All at once she recognized the horses on the far side of the highway. Two blood bays meandered along, munching hay with the rest of the Phantom's herd.

On the near side of the highway, right in her path if she continued on this trail, Sam saw five more horses, a buckskin and several bays including that leggy colt with a white patch over his eye. Their heads flew up and their nostrils fluttered as they inspected Chip.

Horror swept over Sam like a crashing wave. The herd was divided by the highway. Startled by a passing car or truck, they'd reunite.

Every moment of their lives had told them safety was in the herd. No one had taught them to look both ways for traffic.

Think, Sam told herself. Should she try to get them back together now, before something scared them?

And where was Queen? All she needed was for the dun to show up and run gathering laps around her band.

All at once, Sam felt the odd static that came with a lightning storm.

The sky changed from gray to an eerie red and a splashing sound drew Sam's attention to her left. For a minute, she couldn't tell what made the splash. Sun filtered through the clouds and shone on the river, turning it red. Then she saw Queen, scattering red drops as she ran through the shallows of La Charla.

More hooves drew Sam's attention away from Queen and up the stair-step mesas leading to the Calico Mountains.

A big paint with red-brown spots on a creamy body raced toward the divided herd and Sam knew from the animal's determined stride that a new lead mare had been crowned.

Beyond her, the Phantom came down from his ridge top lookout.

His flowing mane and tail caught the ruddy light as he moved down the hillside. This time, he didn't float. There was an urgency to his gait that frightened Sam.

Queen saw it, too. She splashed out of the river and ran clumsily toward the five horses on the near side of the highway. Suddenly she stopped, but Sam didn't think she was daunted by the paint mare.

Queen stood on three legs, calling sharply to the herd. Relieved but full of pity, Sam knew the dun would not be leaving with the herd. The horses glanced at Queen, but did not obey.

Suddenly, every horse stood alert, but they weren't heeding the new lead mare or the Phantom. The sound of an engine warned Sam to look up the highway.

Linc Slocum's beige Cadillac led a motorcade of three black limousines. They would come between the horses in about a minute.

Sam knew what she had to do.

Now, before the cars reached this stretch of road flanked by mustangs, she had to get the herd together.

But it meant riding at a run on Chip.

It meant riding across asphalt.

It meant possible entanglement with Queen, the paint, and the Phantom as they tried to gather the herd at the same time she was.

Fear of falling gripped Sam until the instant the Phantom's neigh rang louder than the approaching cars.

Sam sighed. Long ago, she'd vowed to help the silver stallion and his herd stay safe and free. She had to keep her promise.

As the five wild horses nearest to her drifted in indecision, she set Chip after them. Awkward but strong-minded, Queen closed on this half of the herd as well.

Sam felt Chip's sureness as he noticed he had a herding partner.

Up the highway, Slocum slowed his car to a crawl. Behind him, one limousine stopped and two men in suits disembarked to watch as the buckskin skittered.

"Don't fall, please don't fall," Sam begged.

The blood bays on the far side of the highway surged forward to meet the buckskin, but the big paint mare cut them off her body, then scolded with an angry whinny.

That left four horses on this side. With the buckskin across, she thought the bays might follow, but they were confused. With halting insistence, Queen moved up behind them and nipped at their tails.

If Slocum's motorcade just stayed where it was, everything should be fine.

The three bays bolted across the asphalt, lifting their hooves high from the strange footing.

"All right." Sam sighed, but the bay colt hesitated. It looked away from the herd, as if it heard or smelled something enticing from the direction of the ranches.

"C'mon, baby," Sam said, clucking at him.

The bay colt startled, but in the end, it was Queen who herded him across.

As the last horse crossed to safety, she ignored the applauding onlookers and followed.

The paint mare left no questions about who was in charge. With flashing teeth and flattened ears, she swooped around the latecomers and scolded them into joining the herd.

Sam searched for the Phantom. He was still moving toward her, still more worried than she expected.

Sam heard a roar of acceleration as the cars tried to make up for the time they'd lost to the crossing mustangs.

What is the big hurry? she wondered, but she was more interested in watching the Phantom. Something was clearly wrong.

The stallion dashed toward her, the jostling herd parting around him.

Behind her, Slocum honked his horn. At first,

Sam thought it was in celebration for the sponta-
neous rodeo witnessed by his guests. But when she
twisted in the saddle, Sam felt sick.

The bay colt had turned back, and the Phantom
was sprinting after him.

Chapter Nineteen

𝒯rembling with the need to do what she'd always done, Queen started after the bay colt. Queen didn't care that the Phantom was already on his way. She didn't know, as Sam did, that if the colt could be rescued, the stallion would do it.

The colt would obey the Phantom, but would Queen obey her? Sam knew she could only do her best, and hope.

Sam used Chip like a cutting horse, darting back and forth, keeping Queen cut off from the road. For seconds, they were an even match. Nose to nose, both horses swung together as Queen searched for a way past the big gelding.

Afraid she'd fall, but more afraid she'd lose Queen, Sam leaned forward to grab Queen's headstall, and missed.

"Queen!"

Trying to stay in the saddle, Sam looked over her

shoulder for the voice, then glanced back at the red tiger dun. Head on high, Queen watched Callie lope up on Ace.

"There's my girl," Callie crooned.

Queen didn't go to her, but she didn't run, either. Now, while the mare was distracted by Callie, Sam made a second attempt to snag the mare's lead rope.

She got it.

The mare pulled back, nearly jerking Sam from the saddle. *Dally*! She reminded herself to wind the lead rope around her saddle horn as quickly as she could. If Jake had been able to do that, he wouldn't have lost Queen the first time.

So, though she was off balance, she wrapped the rope around the saddle horn and the mare stopped, blowing. She didn't look as bereft as she had a few minutes ago, though. And it was all because of Callie. The mare was irritated that she couldn't join her herd, but her gaze kept returning to the girl with the bright yellow hair.

Sam met Callie's eyes and gestured for her to come closer. Ace was every bit as good a cow horse as Chip. If Callie rode up and took the lead rope, it should be easier to get the mare back to River Bend.

Callie obeyed Sam's silent summons. She took the lead rope and held tight.

Queen didn't seem to notice. Her attention was fixed on the Phantom as he moved toward the highway.

On shaky legs, the colt faced the car. His body quivered and he was scarcely breathing by the time the Phantom reached him.

The stallion's heavy hooves clacked on the asphalt as he approached the colt.

Seeing a second horse in his way, Slocum honked again.

Sam shuddered at Slocum's arrogance. She could see into the car as Slocum's form leaned forward, blowing a long maddening blast on the horn.

The sound frightened the colt toward his mother, neighing from the tight-gathered band, but the Phantom didn't follow.

Moving with menacing slowness, the stallion squared off with Slocum's Cadillac.

Hurry, get out of the road, Sam thought. *Zanzibar, you can't fight a car.*

The stallion rose on his hind legs, a huge silver thundercloud of a horse, and Sam could tell what Slocum probably didn't suspect. The Phantom wasn't frightened or protective. He was furious. His neigh was the angry trumpeting of a stallion warning back a noisy intruder.

Showing off for his guests, Slocum jumped out of the Cadillac.

"Get outta here! Go on! Move it!"

Majestic and strong, acting as if he'd claimed this highway for his own, the stallion refused to move.

A laugh came from one of the men watching from

outside the limousine. Another man focused a camera on Slocum's stand-off with a wild horse.

The stallion ignored the other men, but Slocum couldn't. He took a step toward the Phantom, waving his arms.

It was a serious mistake.

The stallion came down from his rear, steadied himself. He lowered his head in a snaking, herding motion and darted toward Slocum, mouth agape.

Slocum yelped and hopped back into his car. An instant later, Sam heard the automatic door locks clicking into place.

Sam realized she'd been holding her breath, as she finally released it.

"That's him, isn't it." Callie wasn't really asking a question. "The Phantom."

When Sam nodded, she felt as if a spell had been broken. Few people had been so close to the great silver stallion, and Callie's tone said she was in awe of what she'd just seen. And now, the stallion was coming closer.

Shaking his dished head as if he'd just disciplined a wayward foal, the Phantom trotted off the highway.

As he approached, he tossed his forelock from his eyes.

"Hey boy," Sam whispered, and she could have sworn the stallion's brown eyes shone with good humor. "Yeah, you showed him, boy. Now you'd better take your family and run for it!"

For a minute, she thought he was about to go, but a snort brought him to a stop.

Queen struck at the earth with one hoof, then gave a low nicker. It wasn't a beseeching call, though. It sounded like a reprimand.

The stallion's surprise was easy to read. He hadn't recognized his lead mare, here among the domestic horses. Now his head turned to one side, unsure.

"What should I do?" Callie's whisper was urgent.

"Hang on," Sam said, as Chip tensed beneath the saddle. "Because here he comes."

Majestic in every muscle, the Phantom glanced at Sam, ignored her mount, and moved closer. Queen walked to the end of her lead rope and waited for him.

The stallion and the red dun touched muzzles. Their nostrils fluttered in recognition and then the Phantom dipped his head. Queen's lips grazed the spot between his ears, touching his tangled forelock. For an instant, both horses stood still, and then the stallion was backing. He pivoted, and bolted toward the rest of the herd.

"I guess that's good-bye," Sam said softly.

"She didn't follow him," Callie said in amazement. "She didn't even try."

The paint mare had already herded most of the mustangs toward the uphill path, and the Phantom trotted after them. Just before he reached the steepest part of the trail, he stopped and looked back.

He gave one long, shivering neigh.

Sam felt her heart respond. She wished she could whinny back, but then she realized the farewell wasn't just for her.

Queen lifted her fine red-dun head and rocked toward the stallion, returning his call. She diidn't pull against the lead rope and she didn't sound sad.

As the Phantom galloped toward the Calico Mountains, Queen leaned against Ace. She stood near enough that Callie could touch her. When the girl did, letting her hand rest light as a feather between the mare's ears, Queen didn't pull away.

Watching, Sam decided Queen recognized the same affection she'd shared with the stallion. She must have, because when Callie touched her, Queen closed her eyes and sighed.

Sam was still harboring serious anger toward Linc Slocum while she was cleaning Ace's stall the next afternoon. She forked fresh straw inside, wondering if Norman White had done anything to punish Slocum.

When she heard a car approaching, she leaned her pitchfork against the barn wall. Dad and Brynna were home.

Their rental car had barely stopped when Brynna jumped out and ran laughing toward Sam.

"Oh my gosh, he did it. Norm White really did it!" Brynna said. Her red braid wagged around her shoulders until she stopped to give Sam a hug.

"Did what?" Sam asked into her new stepmother's shoulder.

Dad was slapping Dallas on the back, smiling, and Sam's curiosity slacked off for just a second. With everyone so happy, they might not notice Queen until Callie arrived with the horse trailer to take her to her new home.

"As we were driving in, just outside of Darton," Brynna explained, "we noticed a man in one of those neon-orange vests people wear when they're picking up trash for the county. Usually, you see kids doing that kind of public service work, but this looked like an adult."

Dad stepped up to put his arm around Sam, and continue the story.

"As we pulled alongside, Brynna shouted, 'Stop! That's a BLM truck.' We slowed down, and sure enough, there was Norman White, walking along the edge of the road with Linc Slocum while he picked up litter."

"Litter?" Sam yelped. She hugged herself in delight. For all the trouble Slocum had caused the mustangs, the millionaire deserved a heavy dose of humiliation.

"Norm told me that in my absence," Brynna's voice imitated Mr. White's snooty tone, "he'd determined that making mustangs vulnerable to vehicular slaughter —"

"Getting hit by a car," Dad put in.

"—certainly counted as harassment under the Free-Roaming Wild Horse and Burro Act, and he was inflicting swift punishment."

"Yep," Dad told them, "Linc said he didn't mind telling me he was feeling lower than a snake's belly in a tire track."

They all turned as the front door opened. Blaze raced toward them and Aunt Sue was right behind.

"Sue," Dad said in astonishment. "I hardly recognized you."

Sam stood speechless. Aunt Sue wore jeans, a turquoise tee-shirt, and an old denim jacket of Gram's that had been hanging on the front porch as long as Sam could remember.

"Welcome back, Wyatt, Brynna," Aunt Sue greeted them both, and her arms moved in an unsure motion, as if she didn't know whether to shake hands or hug.

"Aunt Sue," Sam said finally, "what's up with your outfit?"

"Before I lose my nerve, I want to go for a ride." Aunt's Sue's words came out in a rush. "My suggestion to Callie about feeding Queen an apple was so successful—I mean, the girl literally had that mustang eating out of her hand—that I'm ready to progress one more step."

"I remember Callie," Brynna said slowly. "But who's Queen?"

Sam gulped as Dad said a single word.

"Mustang?"

"I can explain everything, Dad," Sam started.

"Later," Aunt Sue insisted. "I've just had a call from a friend who will simply perish if I'm not at her New Year's Day brunch tomorrow morning. So, I plan to hop in my minivan within the hour, but before that—"

"You want to ride Sweetheart," Sam said, suddenly.

"Yes. I want to say good-bye to my sister," Aunt Sue said. She looked at Dad, silently asking permission.

"It'll take us ten minutes to get all saddled up, but I could use a ride," Dad said.

"So could I," Brynna said carefully. "If you don't mind."

"I think that would be fine," Aunt Sue agreed.

Within minutes, Brynna had saddled a rat-tailed Appaloosa named Jeepers-Creepers. Dad was astride Nike and Ace was shifting impatiently as he waited for Sam to help Aunt Sue mount Sweetheart.

"Your left toe goes in there," Sam said, holding the stirrup. "Now bounce a little and throw—"

Quicker than Sam could speak, Aunt Sue was in the saddle. She shifted a little, then straightened her spine and picked up her reins.

"Great!" Sam said. "How'd you know how to do that so well?"

"I didn't bring those binoculars for show, dear," Aunt Sue said. "Every time you mounted up, I was watching."

There was a moment of silence once Sam was in the saddle, too.

"Louise always liked the ridge trail," Dad said.

Sam twisted in her saddle. "I didn't know that."

Dad shrugged. "Said she liked keeping an eye on home, even when she was away from it."

Sam led the way on Ace, and Sweetheart tucked right in behind her stablemate. As Sam looked back over her shoulder, she saw Brynna reach across the space between Jeepers and Nike and take Dad's hand.

Brynna wore a sweet, satisfied smile as Dad lifted her hand and kissed it.

Sam blinked away happy tears. It was the last day of an old year that had held lots of trouble, but even more excitement and happiness.

Queen and Callie were forming their own new family. The Phantom was safe in his hidden valley with a new lead mare to help run the herd. And down here at River Bend . . .

Sam looked back over her shoulder at the white ranch house with green shutters, just as Dad had said her mother used to do.

She sighed and gave Ace's smooth neck a pat. Here at River Bend, everything was going to be just fine.

From
Phantom Stallion
~∂ 8 ∂~
GOLDEN GHOST

"Remind me not to go into the mines while we're in Nugget," Sam said.

"Mine shafts aren't exactly my favorite places to begin with," Jen said. "Besides, my dad says Nugget is haunted."

"I was really hoping you wouldn't say that." Sam moaned.

"Why? Neither of us believes it's true."

Sam felt a hum of tension along her nerves. Of course she didn't think it was true, but why had Jen even brought it up?

Just then, a high-pitched sound made both horses hesitate.

Silly froze, ears pricked straight and trembling.

"What was that?" Sam said quietly.

"A bird?" Jen offered.

"But it sounded like—" Sam began. She closed her lips. It sounded like a flute. A bone flute of the sort used in Native American ceremonies. But that was impossible.

Suddenly, Jen pointed and Sam looked ahead.

At first, Sam saw a wavering pool of light. She

couldn't have said whether it was silver or gold, water or molten metal. She only knew the flash hurt her eyes with its brilliance. A village was turned upside down in the midst of it.

Talk about impossible! She blinked and squinted. That splash of radiance was pretty far off. She focused hard. No, it wasn't that far away. Perhaps a mile.

For a second, Sam told herself she should have eaten breakfast before she rode out this morning. Gram vowed Sam's brain would work better if she ate.

But hunger and distance couldn't explain what she saw next.

Fairy light and golden, a palomino horse flickered across the playa, danced through a row of upside-down houses—and vanished.